TRO

THE ELSKER SAGA

S.T. Bende

The Elsker Saga
Tro
Copyright © 2013, S.T. Bende
Edited by: Lauren McKellar and Eden Plantz
Interior Snowflakes by: Eden Plantz
Cover Art by: Alerim
ISBN: 1502701308
ISBN-13: 978-1502701305

First publication: 2013, S.T. Bende

DEDICATION

To my biggest little blessings: may your faith in your
dreams be every bit as strong as my faith in you.
To the man who has blessed my life with
faith, hope, and love.
And to everyone who fell for a Norse god—
this one's for you.

CONTENTS

Chapter One   Pg 7

Chapter Two   Pg 17

Chapter Three   Pg 33

Chapter Four   Pg 48

Chapter Five   Pg 60

Chapter Six   Pg 71

Chapter Seven   Pg 83

Chapter Eight   Pg 100

Chapter Nine   Pg 114

Chapter Ten   Pg 124

Chapter Eleven   Pg 140

Chapter Twelve   Pg 152

Chapter Thirteen   Pg 161

Chapter Fourteen   Pg 174

Chapter Fifteen   Pg 185

Chapter Sixteen   Pg 200

Chapter Seventeen   Pg 220

Chapter Eighteen   Pg 229

CHAPTER ONE

"Down you fall, into a sleep;
Monsters all, with you, shall creep.
Demons joyful, spirits fly,
For the gods, at last, shall die.
Goodnight little ones."

THE SHROUDED FIGURE FINISHED *the macabre lullaby on a sharp note, her scratchy voice reverberating through the otherwise quiet nursery. She clutched three bundles as she stood. Her silhouette easily stood twenty feet in height; she made an imposing figure against the arched window. She crossed the room with awkward strides to deposit each bundle in a crib. With the babies safely distributed, she moved to the rocking chair and touched one gnarled finger to a piece of paper. Her eyes were hooded, but even in the semi-darkness, I could see the joy behind them. Her mouth curved into a menacing smile, yellow teeth* *poking at sharp angles against purple lips.*

"Sleep well, my little darlings," she croaked. "Your prophecy is a thing of beauty. The Fates expect great things of you." She dropped the paper onto the chair and walked out of the room, directing an eerie smile at each crib as she left. Then she closed the door tightly behind her.

I crept toward the note on silent feet, careful not to disturb anything more than the air. It was a cavernous room with forty-foot ceilings, and heavy tapestries that lined the walls. Three cribs sat beneath an imposing chandelier. The three bundles slept peacefully, their hushed breathing the room's only sound. But the bundles weren't making the kinds of cooing sleep sounds I'd expect of newborns.

Now they were stirring, the movement loosening the bindings on their swaddles. Their faces were still obscured in shadow, but I was struck by the unnerving realization that these babies were nothing like human babies. One let out a guttural hiss; the other a soft growl. And the third made a noise so animalistic, it sounded like a wail ... or a war cry.

As the cacophony in the nursery reached a fevered pitch, I darted for the rocking chair. Without thinking I grabbed the note and stuffed it in my pocket, then I made a dash for the door. Whatever those babies were, I didn't want to be around them any longer.

My hand burned as I turned the knob. I jumped back, cradling my fingers. The skin pulled across my bone; large blisters had already begun to form. Someone, or something had turned the metal molten.

Maybe it was a defensive spell, something to protect the children. With any luck, I'd never know. I pushed through the pain and gripped the doorknob again, wrenching it open and bolting down the hallway. I ignored the searing ache in my palms as I pumped my arms, willing myself to reach the exit faster.

Heavy footsteps thudded behind me. They were slow but determined, each step closing the distance between my pursuer and me. I didn't have to turn around to know an angry giantess was bearing down, and I didn't want to think about what she'd do if she caught up.

Ducking my head, I tore around a corner and bolted for the doorway. It was close, only ten yards away. When I was halfway there, two heavily armed guards stepped into my path. They were easily thirty-feet tall, each with an array of weapons attached to a thick belt. One held a spear in his hand, while the other wielded a broad sword. Both locked me in their sights and charged. My head whipped back and forth—the angry mother closed in on me from behind. The guards were fast approaching from ahead. My only option was to hide.

I turned on my heel and bolted through the closest doorway. Now I was in some kind of recreation room with large chairs, a blazing fireplace, and, thankfully, high windows, flanked by thick curtains. My legs burned as I dove behind one, curling into a ball and willing my breath to come in quiet gasps. It might have bought me a minute, tops, but a minute was all I would need.

Thundering footsteps announced the giants' entry. They crossed the room with angry shouts. The language was foreign but the sentiment translated easily enough. A few more seconds, and I would be deader than a doornail.

My blistered palm wrapped around my grandmother's necklace as I squeezed my eyes shut. I drew on my happiest memory of my sinfully gorgeous husband, Ull. Just that morning he'd stood at the altar of the little church in Cardiff. He'd been the most beautiful creature I'd ever laid eyes on, watching me walk up the aisle with near-worshipful eyes. The smile playing on his lips and the gratitude in his gaze were images I'd remember for the rest of my existence—no matter how short it might be. The footsteps stopped just beyond my reach, and I knew the guards had found me. It was only a matter of time before they ripped down the curtains and eliminated the threat.

Hopefully, it would be over quickly. Pain had always been my undoing.

The silver replica of Thor's hammer began to warm in my hand, and I opened my eyes. Beams of light radiated from between my fingers in bright flashes. They were sure to give away my location, but I didn't care. I knew exactly what was happening.

It was taking me home.

I squeezed my necklace as the guards tore down the curtains. The beams increased in intensity, striking the guards in the chest and throwing them back. The angry giantess stormed across the room, hands outstretched and ready to strike. Before she could reach me, I was sucked into the air, my insides churning under the unbearable pressure as I hurtled through darkness. My *bones felt like they might rip clear out of my body, and the pounding in my head was so insistent I danced precariously along the edge of consciousness. Just before I could pass out, I remembered the note. I tore it from my pocket as I hurtled through space, determined to see its contents before I woke up from this bizarre vision. My gut told me the scene I was in was old; I was intruding on a nightmare from a long ago past. And I had a feeling I'd need to know what that note said in order to protect our future.*

The paper shook in my hands as I strained to make out the words. This prophecy would spell the fate of the three babies. It would explain why their giantess mother was overjoyed at its news; and why my very presence had driven her to a rage. Whatever it was, whatever their fates, my gut told me the prophecy and those children had deep ties to my new family.

I unfolded the note. Hastily scrawled letters told the future of the three newborns from the nursery. The prophecy marked a new beginning that necessitated a violent end. It contained only two words.

End Asgard.

I closed my eyes as the bile rose thick in my throat. And then I was consumed by darkness.

❄ ❄ ❄ ❄

"Sweetheart. Wake up." The voice in my ear was soft yet commanding; the words managed to be both a plea and an order. My eyelids fluttered, and I buried my face against the warmth beside me. It smelled of earth, and pine.

It smelled like home.

11

"Wake up *now*, Kristia." The warmth moved away from my cheek, and when I dragged my eyes open I found myself cradled in strong arms. The magnificent blond deity looking down at me had a furrowed brow, set jaw, and the perma-stubble that was so characteristically Ull. Even on his wedding day, he couldn't bring himself to shave.

"Hi," I murmured as I rubbed the sleep from my lids. All thoughts of my nightmare were instantly forgotten as I lost myself in my brand-spankin'-new husband's endless blue eyes.

"Hi yourself." Ull brushed a lock of hair off my face and lifted me so I was positioned tightly against him. "Must have been some dream."

"Hmm?" I dragged myself away from the whirlpool that was Ull's gaze, and absorbed my surroundings. Opulent couches equipped with seatbelts, a small table holding half-empty champagne flutes, and an entertainment unit that would rival my fantasy of a Hollywood screening room. Asgard's private jet was equal parts elegance and comfort, and right now it was barreling toward the mysterious destination where Ull and I would spend the first night of our married life.

Oh, God. Our wedding night. I swallowed hard as I tried not to over-think that one.

"Are you cold?" Ull reached behind him to pull a blanket over my bare legs. The skirt of my going-away dress had inched up another few centimeters, so it barely covered the tops of my thighs. Now the expanse of exposed flesh was being massaged by Ull's rather sizeable palm.

I flushed. "Not anymore."

"Good." Ull leaned down to press his cheek to my forehead. "Now, are you going to tell me why you were yelling in your sleep? Did you have another vision?"

I struggled to remember the images that must have troubled my dreams. But for the first time, something had slipped through the normally firm grip of my subconscious. Flashes of colors came to mind— dark purples, menacing crimson; and feelings— desolation, fear, and . . . joy? That made no sense. Those feelings went together as well as peanut butter and pickles.

"I don't know what I was dreaming about." I shook my head. "I can't remember it."

Ull's brow furrowed against mine. "Is this common? Have you forgotten your dreams before?"

"Not that I can think of. Usually they're right there when I wake up." I shrugged. "Must not have been important, I guess."

"You were screaming." Ull spoke softly. "You sounded afraid."

"Really?" I squeezed my eyes shut and tried to force the dream back into my consciousness. But it was gone, filtered from my memories like water through a fishing-net. "Sorry. I have nothing."

I opened my eyes and blinked at Ull. He was frowning at me.

"I do not have to stress to you the importance of your visions. If they—"

"I know." My fingers grazed his arm.

"You are the Seer—and now that you are immortal, this makes you Asgard's strongest defense. If whatever you envisioned is something that might come to fruition, it is imperative that you share it with me."

"Sorry, Ull. I've really got nothing." I shook my head. "You know I'd tell you if I could."

"If you think of anything, *anything*—"

"I know." I raised a finger to stroke the stubble along his jaw. "I'll tell you right away. You know you don't have to worry about me all the time."

"Kristia, you are my world. Of course I worry."

I sighed. Ull was innately protective—his position as an Asgardian warrior gave him every right to expect the worst could happen to the people he loved. But ever since our favorite Norn, Elsker, had declared I was this long-prophesied visionary the gods dubbed the Seer, he'd taken protective to a whole new level. Because I was privy to visions of the past, present, and future, I was the shiniest new weapon in Asgard's arsenal. I was also one of our enemies' most highly sought-after targets. And with everything we'd just been through, my six-foot, five-inch, immortal assassin was terrified that somebody would take me away from him.

It was kind of adorable.

"Is there any chance we could just enjoy our honeymoon?" I moved my finger along Ull's jaw, over his Adam's apple, and down the hollow of his neck. My palm rested against his chest; the thud of his heart beat a steady rhythm against my skin. "Please?"

"That look is not going to work on me every time, you know." Ull sounded frustrated.

"Then why is the corner of your mouth twitching?"

"Because. That look *is* going to work on me ninety nine percent of the time, and you know it." Ull chuckled. "All right. I will drop it. But only because we are here."

"We are?" I leaned across Ull's lap and tried to raise the window shade.

"Not yet. Trust me, you want to see the whole picture. Not just a sliver of it." He tightened his arms around my shoulders as the plane touched down. In seconds it came to a stop, and the world's loveliest flight attendant walked out of the cockpit. She pressed a button on the side of the plane and a door opened, inviting beams of sunlight into the dim cabin. It was a shock after spending several hours in semi-darkness, and I blinked against the brightness.

"Sorry sweetheart." Ull reached into my bag, then placed a pair of sunglasses atop my nose. He cupped my cheek in one hand. "I forget how sensitive your eyes must be."

It was true. Enhanced vision was just one of the side effects of becoming a goddess. But if the sparks shooting off my cheek were any indication, my sensitivity to Ull's touch was going to be much more problematic.

"Come." Ull stood. After the wedding he'd changed into a black suit and a crisp button down, but sometime during the flight he'd ditched his coat. Now he smoothed the front of his pants, stretched his long legs and held out a hand. I wound my fingers through his and followed him to the front of the plane, tugging at the hem of my dress as I moved. "Leave it," Ull ordered without looking back. "I like it up there."

The temperature in my cheeks tripled.

"Mr. and Mrs. Myhr." Our flight attendant tossed her chocolaty-brown hair over one shoulder. "Welcome to Asgard Cay."

"Thank you, Stacey." Ull nodded as he stepped out of the plane. He reached into his pocket and pulled out a pair of aviator shades. He put them on, and turned to me, hand outstretched. "Are you ready?"

There was no way I could ever be ready for this— my first day as an immortal, starting my honeymoon with a Norse god. So I did the only thing I could. I closed my eyes, took a breath, and put my hand in his. Then I stepped out of the cabin.

"Let's do this."

CHAPTER TWO

ULL WASN'T KIDDING WHEN he said he was taking me somewhere remote. We were right in the middle of Odin-knows-where, surrounded by pristine turquoise water on all sides. The jet was parked on a landing strip that looked out of place on a stretch of pink sand. It was the only thing on the narrow patch of land; a boat docked thirty yards away would be our transportation to the foliage-rich island in the distance.

"Where are we?" I kept my weight on my toes as I followed Ull across the grainy sand. The designer stilettos Victoria had gifted me might have been the "*it*" shoe of the season, but they weren't exactly the best beachwear. I breathed a sigh of relief when we reached the dock, stepping over the gaps between boards as Ull loaded our suitcases onto the boat.

"Asgard Cay, the Firm's private island and resident safe house in this quadrant of Midgard."

Ull hummed as he worked. When the boat was loaded, he turned to me with an impish smile. "Get in here." His hands easily circled my waist and he lifted me into the boat before jumping in after me.

"You're in a good mood."

Ull raised an eyebrow. "Like you said. It is time to enjoy our honeymoon."

I ducked behind a wall of blonde hair so Ull wouldn't see my blush. "Drive, Myhr."

"As you wish."

Ull steered effortlessly, whistling as the boat cut through the smooth water. His eyes sparkled from beneath his aviators, and even the permanently tense line of his jaw seemed to have relaxed. For the first time since I'd met him, Ull appeared fully at ease.

When we docked on the opposite shore, it was easy to see why. Asgard Cay was a pristine island covered in white sand. Immaculate waters mirrored Ull's irises and lush jungle foliage teemed with colorful birds, loudly singing their greeting. There were no roads, no signs, not even a footprint to make me think there was another human—or god—on the island. Even the jet had taken off, though I hadn't heard its quiet departure over the motor of the boat.

Ull tossed our luggage on the dock, bending to lift me onto the planks. He kept me tightly in one hand, our luggage in the other, and walked toward a house set in from the water's edge.

"Home sweet home." Ull grinned.

Cue the understatement police.

I took in the Paleolithic jungle plants framing the

grand wooden structure, the oversized shutters guarding each wide-paned window, and the bright tropical flowers and tiki torches lining the path from ocean to front step. The far side of the home backed into the foliage, while the front of the veranda led directly onto the pale sand of the beach. It was absolutely breathtaking.

"Do all your residences look like this?"

"No." Ull stopped walking. "Some are bigger."

I raised my eyes to the heavens. "Well this one is lovely."

"Not compared to you." Ull let the words linger between us, and my cheeks blazed anew. Apparently becoming an Asgardian had done diddly-squat for my inability to hide emotions. Ull touched my flaming face with a smile. "I have never seen anything more beautiful than you wearing that dress, walking to join me at the alter."

"So you liked my dress?"

"Yes. But I liked what it symbolized more." Ull didn't have to explain. He'd spent his existence thinking he was destined to live alone. It baffled him that I'd willingly traded my mortality for what he saw as a near certain-death sentence. Ragnarok loomed on the horizon, and it promised to end the Norse pantheon once and for all. But what Ull could never understand was that immortality with him, even if it only lasted a few months, was infinitely more valuable to me than one hundred years of being human. Ull was my world, and nothing was going to keep me from enjoying every single minute I got to spend at his side.

"Come on, handsome. I want to see the house."

-Ull dropped the luggage and carried me across the threshold before setting me gently on my feet. I walked across the smooth wooden boards, taking in the open floor-plan. The living area stretched in front of me, large windows looking to the beach beyond. The kitchen sat behind the living area, with a large island-top and barstools separating the two. The bedrooms were off to each side, their imposing teak doors left open just enough to allow a glimpse of the key pieces of furniture. Ull kissed my cheek, pointed me to the master, and left to bring our suitcases into the house. When his glorious posterior disappeared from view, I closed my eyes for a beat. Gathering all my courage, I opened them, walked to the nearest door and stepped through. And then I forgot to breathe.

The master suite was as opulent as I would expect for an Asgardian retreat. The dark wooden floors continued through this room, ending at the cream-colored walls that were easily fifteen feet high. A wide fan blew air down from the ceiling, keeping the heat at bay, but my eyes were locked on the room's most prominent feature: the enormous bed swathed in netting, with plush white linen covering the generous surface. My insides tumbled as I thought about what was going to happen on that bed.

Oh, good gravy.

I forced myself to focus on the mahogany dresser, nightstands, and armoire. I spent a solid half-minute staring at the French doors that opened onto the deck, with three steps leading to the white sand below.

But my eyes kept returning to the bed. It was the sun to my Icarus; as much as it frightened me, I was completely drawn to it.

"Do you like the room?" Ull's deep baritone came from the doorway and I turned with a gasp. "I am sorry—I thought you heard me come in."

A nervous giggle passed my lips as my eyes darted between the god and the bed. "I was just . . . uh . . ." I flailed. There were no words.

Ull raised one eyebrow. "How about I make dinner while you get changed. Gorgeous as it is, I cannot imagine that dress is well suited for the beach."

I nodded, one nervous head bob. Ull smiled, then tilted his head toward the bathroom.

"You might recognize the shower. I had it modeled after Ýdalir's."

A soak under hot water sounded like a *great* idea. "Sold."

Ull took a step toward the bathroom. "Would you like any company?"

My eyes doubled in size. "Um. I. I mean . . ." Oh, Lord. I knew this was coming, but now? My legs hadn't been shaved in a good twenty hours.

Ull let out a throaty chuckle. "Too soon. Got it. Well then, meet me on the verandah in half an hour. I will be the one grilling chicken."

"Where did we get chicken?" While I'd been appreciating the house's solitude, I hadn't stopped to think about where we could pick up eggs or milk. Or chicken.

"One of the junior Valkyries delivered food this morning. I gave Freya a list of our favorite meals and she made sure the kitchen was stocked. If she followed my instructions, there should be an entire shelf of your Caramel McVitie's." Ull shot me a grin. "If you notice anything I missed just let me know and I will have it brought in."

"First of all, thank you for the McVitie's. That was seriously great of you. And second, battle goddesses do your grocery shopping?"

Ull shrugged. "A trainee is supposed to be permanently stationed at Ýdalir, but I had Freya reassign her."

"Do all gods have Valkyries to do that kind of thing for them?"

"All of the royal bloodline does." Ull touched my arm and my skin warmed instantly. "I just opted out of the service."

"The royal . . . oh." I blinked. "Right. Odin. Then Thor. Then you."

"Then us," Ull corrected.

"Us. Of course." I'd married into Asgardian royalty, and immortal warriors were tasked with picking up my perishables. "Well if it's all the same to you, I'd rather we do our own grocery shopping back home."

"I concur. A little privacy goes a long way." Ull trailed his finger down the back of my hand, leaving a trail of sparks in his wake. It felt like I'd been shocked. I jumped away, then shook my head. If I didn't get control over my nerve endings soon, this honeymoon was going to be all kinds of embarrassing.

"Sorry," I murmured, stepping back into Ull's arms. "My skin's still a little over sensitive."

"There is no need to apologize. This must all seem very overwhelming. What do you say I leave you to your shower? Dinner will be waiting when you are ready." Ull stepped out of the room, pausing in the doorway to give me a wink. "I do think you will appreciate the setup in there."

"Can't wait." I smiled, then grabbed my toiletry bag and scurried into the bathroom. Ull hadn't been wrong—this room was every bit as magnificent as Ull's bath at Ýdalir, with a generous six-headed shower and a separate jet-filled bathtub.

My fingers were clammy as I undid the buttons on my dress and slid it off my shoulders. It fluttered to the floor, the beads clinking softly on the tile. With a twist of the knob, warm water rained from the showerheads. I stepped into the enclosure with a sigh. Steady streams hit my body from all sides. I let the warmth work through my stiff muscles, then reached for my toiletry bag and pulled out my razor. When I'd washed away eight hours of flight time, I grabbed a fluffy towel from the heated rack, and stepped out of the shower.

I wasn't sure what appropriate honeymoon attire was for a newly-anointed goddess on a private Asgardian island, so I grabbed a white sundress and gold strappy sandals, and hoped for the best. Then I shook my hair free from its messy half-updo, and tied it into a loose braid. As an afterthought, I took a hibiscus from the bowl by the sink and pinned it over my ear, then I sent a silent prayer to any god listening. There was no turning back now.

I padded across the hardwood floors and out to the wraparound deck. Ull had set a table for two, complete with flickering tapers in silver candlesticks. I smiled shyly as he held out a chair. Somewhere along the way, he'd changed into island apparel too. He looked more beautiful than any human ever could. His thighs strained against khaki shorts that fell to his knees, and his white linen shirt was mostly unbuttoned, rendering my imagination useless. Thick, blond hair flopped over his eyes as he laid a plate of jerk chicken on the table, and I caught a whiff of that impossibly heady, woodsy smell from his bare chest. I was torn between my desire to eat the delicious meal he'd prepared and an altogether different and much more embarrassing desire.

If Ull sensed my mood he was too refined to say anything. We were starving after our long flight, so there wasn't much room for conversation anyway.

Ull was a good cook, and I quickly finished two portions of chicken. When I set my utensils diagonally across my plate, he stood with a slow smile.

"Shall we?" He reached out, and I took his hand. Fingers entwined, we walked down to the beach. A mild breeze caressed my skin, soothing the burn brought on by Ull's touch. I sent calming thoughts to my palms, and the burn went away. My new Asgardian skin was going to get a stern talking-to if it didn't stop overwhelming me with every touch. But I had a feeling Ull's touches would always overwhelm me. I wouldn't have wanted it any other way.

We kicked off our sandals and waded just far enough in the ocean so it lapped against our calves. The water was bath-temperature, despite the setting sun, and I relished the feeling of warmth that settled over me. Ull and I stood hand in hand, our feet buried in soft sand beneath the waves. We watched in silence as the sun dipped below the horizon, and the stars came out in the darkening sky. The full moon reflected off the water as Ull slowly turned his body to face mine. My heart accelerated to twice its normal pace and I shifted from one foot to the other. Ull's eyes smoldered beneath unnaturally long lashes, leaving no doubt as to his intentions.

I dropped my gaze.

"Ull, I . . ." I broke off. I had no idea how to do this.

"Hey." Ull lifted my chin with one finger. I had no choice but to look at him. "It is just me."

"I know, but . . ." I bit my bottom lip. There was absolutely no accounting for my sudden anxiety. It made zero sense that the thing I'd spent months all but begging for was the thing that suddenly had my palms sweating.

"I get it," Ull whispered. He put his hand on the back of my head and pulled me against his chest. "Me too."

We didn't move for a long moment; we just stood knee-deep in the water, Ull's hands cradling me to him while I took slow breaths to stop the jackrabbit executing a tap routine in my chest. When it became apparent the jackrabbit was planning several encores,

I balled Ull's shirt in my hands. *Get a grip, Kristia.*

"How about I tell you a story?" Ull rested his chin on the top of my head.

My lips moved against his chest. "Okay."

"Once upon a time in Asgard, there was a god named Freyr. Freyr was the god of, among other things, fertility."

I blushed. "I remember." Ull's grandmother Olaug had given me a mildly inappropriate wedding gift in Freyr's likeness. Something about wanting grandbabies . . .

"Right." Ull chuckled. "Well, in time, the god of fertility got lonely. He moped around Asgard, and made everyone around him miserable. Our sea god, Njord, could not take it any longer, so he asked Freyr's servant, Skirnir, to find out what was wrong. Freyr answered that he had seen a woman—one so beautiful that when she raised her arms, the light bounced off her skin and the whole world brightened. Skirnir asked why this made Freyr sad, and Freyr answered simply, 'Because I cannot be with her.' The woman was Gerd, the daughter of mountain giants, and relationships between the races were deeply discouraged."

Boy, oh boy, had I been there.

"Freyr was consumed—he thought of nothing but Gerd, and he knew he would die if he could not have her. He was far too infatuated to be bothered with something as trifling as Asgardian law, or proprietal convention, so he asked Skirnir to bring Gerd to him. Skirnir agreed, on the condition that Freyr lend him his sword."

"That doesn't seem like a huge deal," I pointed out. The water lapped around my knees as I shifted my weight.

"In most cases, it would not be. But Freyr's sword had magical properties; some said it fought of its own will. To lose such a weapon, even for a short time, would put Freyr in grave danger. But his love for Gerd meant more to him than his own survival, and he willingly handed over his weapon and risked his life so they could be together."

"What happened?"

"When news of Freyr's vulnerability got out, his enemies swarmed. But the god had something worth fighting for. And when Gerd appeared, nine nights after Freyr sent for her, they were married. They have lived together happily ever since."

My lips curved up against the lines of Ull's chest. "That's a really nice story."

"It is."

Ull put his hands on my arms and gently pushed me away. When I looked up, his face bore a reverence that sent warmth shooting through me. Even though my feet were planted firmly in wet sand, I swayed just a smidge. How was it possible this spectacular deity could see me the way he did?

"What Freyr felt for Gerd, what he was willing to risk for her, was not even a hundredth of what I feel for you. I love you, Kristia Myhr. There is no one else I have ever wanted to share my life with. From the moment you walked into that museum, you have been my world, and nothing gives me greater pleasure than knowing I get to spend an eternity with you at my side."

The moisture that was building in my eyes escaped, and I pressed the heel of my hand against the top of my cheek to slow the tears. "Ull," I murmured. Then I wrapped my fingers through his tousled locks and pulled his face to mine. The strands twined around my wedding band and I tugged gently, crushing his lips against my own. His taste was intoxicating, a spicy blend of mint and wood that was overwhelming and familiar all at the same time.

I stepped closer so that only our clothing separated us. The movement caused the water to lap against the backs of my knees. Ull ran one hand down my ribcage, settling it firmly around my waist. The sensation sent a wave of heat coursing through me, and I stood on tiptoes to deepen the contact. My tongue pressed against his, the languid dance draining the blood from my head to somewhere entirely less appropriate. I let out a soft sigh as the sensation overtook me, pressing my chest against Ull's and wanting to eliminate any possible distance between us.

God, how I loved this god.

Ull groaned, a hushed sound that reverberated through his torso. I felt it through the thin fabric of my dress. It tickled my overly sensitive skin, and awakened a longing I'd waited nineteen years to fulfill. Ull was mine. I'd literally laid down my life so we could be together, and I knew he'd go to the ends of the worlds to protect me. There would never be anyone who made me feel the way he did. And there was nobody else I wanted to experience this with. Ever.

I was overwhelmed by the enormity of this moment, but I was ready. Boy, howdy, was I ready.

"Ull." I pulled my lips away long enough to murmur my consent. He cupped my jaw in his enormous palms, and pressed his forehead against mine.

"I will take care of you, Kristia. In this, and in all things."

"I know you will."

And with that, Ull swept me off my feet. Saltwater dripped from my calves as he cradled me in his arms and carried me with otherworldly speed across the beach and through the French doors that led to the master suite. He set me on the oversized bed with the utmost care and gently loosened my braid.

I cupped his face in my hands. "I love you, Ull Myhr."

His eyes turned to inky-blue pools. A shiver worked its way up my back. That color . . . so many good things happened when his eyes turned that color.

"Lay back," Ull commanded. I obeyed. He ran his eyes up my body, pausing when he reached the hemline of my dress. A slow smile played at his lips and my shiver turned to a warm glow. My insides began to hum as Ull raked his gaze along the curve of my hips, over my stomach, pausing again at my chest.

His smile disappeared and the inky-blue pools deepened a shade. They smoldered at the low *V* of my neckline, a look so intense I squirmed under his stare.

My movement broke his focus and he pulled his eyes up to my face. As I watched, my consummate gentleman disappeared and the warrior took over. The veins in Ull's forearms throbbed as he placed his fists on either side of my waist. His jaw was locked, his eyes steely in their focus. His sights were set on a singular goal—a goal I was suddenly desperate to reach.

"Ull," I breathed. I reached up to touch his chin. "Please."

His eyes glazed at the words, and he dropped his head. His lips met the side of my neck. He sucked gently, causing my chest to rise and fall. I hadn't adequately prepared myself for the intensity of the sensation. When Ull had touched me before I'd been changed, it had felt amazing, but I'd always known he'd stop before he reached a certain point. Now, knowing we were going to see this through . . . it altered things. My nerves were one thousand times more highly strung, my skin infinitely more aware, and something inside me had given up any illusion of self-control. A six-foot, five-inch Norse deity hovered over me, and I wanted to be his, in every conceivable way.

Right. Now.

My hands flew up to claw at the fabric of Ull's shirt. Without breaking his kiss he shifted his weight to one fist and ripped his shirt clean off. It sent ripples through the air that brushed my skin as it fluttered to the ground, but I was too distracted to watch its descent. My hands now had total access to the multitude of muscles that made up Ull's back. There were literally hundreds; I could have spent all night exploring them.

But Ull had other ideas.

"Are you particularly fond of this dress?" His voice sounded thick as he lifted his head. His eyes were hazy; I doubted he could see me with any degree of clarity. I also doubted he cared.

"Mmm." I wrapped one hand in his hair and pulled his face back to its rightful spot on my neck. His teeth scraped lightly against my flesh and I gripped the sheet in my free hand. *God, he felt so good.*

"If you like the dress then tell me now." Ull spoke through a clenched jaw. His mouth had made its way down to my neckline. "Because one way or another, it is coming off."

I pushed against him so he was forced onto his back. Without thinking, I rolled over, shimmied out of Victoria's spectacular design, and turned back to Ull. Now I lay on my side in the lacy white lingerie I'd been mortified to receive as a honeymoon gift. Turned out, my flatmates knew *a lot* more than I did.

"*Faen.*" Ull's eyes rolled closed. "You are wearing . . . that is just . . . I cannot . . ."

Ull dropped his head and the stubble of his jaw scratched the tender tissue above my bra. His lips covered the abrasion, hot kisses tracing the lace along the edge. I fisted the sheets, pulling them tight between my fingers to keep from crying out. With a slow exhale, Ull grazed his nose just below the underwire. My entire body shook as the cool air chilled my skin. Every single part of me wanted to belong to him.

As if sensing my thought, Ull shifted so he hovered just on top of me. I pulled him closer, desperate to close the distance between us. He stilled, and I released my grip so I could look at him. When I did, the Asgardian assassin stared me down.

"*Jeg elsker deg*, Kristia," he vowed. He stroked my temple with the back of one finger.

I blinked. "I love you too."

"And I will always take care of you. Always." The fire in Ull's eyes sparked something inside of me. My desire burned, slow at first, then building to the point of pain. I didn't know how much more of this I could take.

"Prove it," I whispered. Ull's eyes turned a shade so dark, they were nearly black.

"Gladly." He covered my mouth with his and I melted under his touch. With a grateful sigh I gave myself over to the unbelievable reality.

I was his.

CHAPTER THREE

AS CONCIOUSNESS SLOWLY OVERCAME me, I felt the filtered sun streaming across my body. I pressed my cheek to the firm surface I was draped across, smiling at the realization it was my husband's impressive torso. Ull's thumb made slow circles across the small of my back as I slowly opened my eyes.

"Good morning. Did you sleep well?"

"Sleep isn't exactly what I remember about last night."

Ull laughed before examining me. "How are you feeling?"

I thought for a moment then answered truthfully, "Really, really happy. How do you feel?"

"I feel nothing but absolute joy. Last night was the most amazing night I have ever experienced. In fact," he raised himself on one arm so that his body rested lightly on mine, "I think I owe you a 'thank you' for showing me exactly what I have been missing all these millennia."

I pulled him closer, a smile glowing between us, ending our brief conversation.

❄ ❄ ❄ ❄

Three days later, Ull taunted me from the beach.

"Are you ready to show me what you are made of, Mrs. Myhr? Or were you planning to lounge around all day?" The mid-morning sun beat down on Ull's unbelieveably delicious torso as he dried himself from his recent swim. Saltwater glistened in tiny pools along his abs, reflecting the light in shimmering patterns. The entire effect was dazzling.

"I believe the purpose of a honeymoon is to lounge around and do very little, so you have energy left over at the end of the day to do more important things." I raised an eyebrow from my chaise.

"I see. So you are not goddess enough to do both. Is that what you are saying?"

He knew I couldn't say no to a challenge.

"Fine. Ask me again."

"I asked if you are ready, Mrs. Myhr."

"Ready to school you, if that's what you mean." I tossed my hat onto the sand and walked toward the water.

"About bloody time," Ull muttered. "I have been waiting an entire week for you to get around to this."

"I'm sorry. Have I not been fulfilling my wifely duties?"

"Not this one." He grinned. "Come on, you have to

be a little curious about what you can do."

Terrified was more like it. So far I'd discovered that my hair kind of glowed, I didn't trip over my own feet anymore, and being married to Ull was hands down the best thing that had ever happened to me. Being a goddess was exceeding all of my expectations. I didn't want to push my luck. Besides, learning about the rest of my abilities would mean I'd have to start preparing for Ragnarok, something I didn't want to deal with when I had so many wonderful distractions on Asgard Cay.

Like the drop-dead gorgeous god standing in his swim trunks, staring me down.

"How about you just tell me what I can do and then we can go back to practicing some of the other stuff we've been doing lately? Especially that one thing we did last night. You know, where you—"

"Tempting though that sounds, no. I want to see what my wife is capable of. How about a little race?" Ull was enjoying this far too much.

"Oh, fine. But when I beat you, you have to bow to me and say 'Kristia, you are the fastest, most graceful, most phenomenal goddess that ever there was.' And then you have to kiss my feet." I waggled my freshly-pedicured toes at him.

"All right. And if I win you have to say 'Ull, Master of my World, you are everything I had ever hoped for and I am so very, very, very, very lucky to have you.' And then you have to make me waffles."

"Four verys?"

"And waffles."

"Deal." I reached behind me to grab my foot. Stretching seemed prudent. "So what do I have to do?"

"Race me. From here to the edge of the forest and back."

I gauged the distance. "About a mile?"

"Give or take." Ull shrugged. "We can make it shorter if you are too chicken."

"Oh, please. You're gonna be so embarrassed when you get whooped by a girl." I talked a big game, but I wasn't sure even my newfound abilities could get me a whole mile without falling flat on my face. Nineteen years of being uncoordinated weren't so easily forgotten.

"Bring it on." Ull drew a line in the sand and crouched behind it. "On your mark. Get set."

"Go!" I bolted half a second ahead of him, pumping my legs as fast as they could go. Energy coiled in my muscles, letting itself out in a gradual stream of power. The power steadily increased as I moved, thrumming just beneath my skin, as if it had been waiting for me to activate it. With each step I seemed to double my speed, practically leaping off the sand as I ran. I drove my arms back and forth, increasing my momentum. It was nuts. I'd never had this kind of agility before.

The soft thud of footfalls on sand pounded just behind me, so I dug in my toes and lowered my head, bearing down with all of my strength. The trees got closer and I skidded to a stop just in time to hear the god behind me do the same. I turned and ran hard in the opposite direction, feeling the wind on my face and the sand kick up behind my heels. This was amazing.

I reached Ull's hand-drawn finish line at the same time he did, and I fell to the ground, peals of delighted laughter ringing across the sand. "That was fun!"

"You cheated." Ull sat next to me and wiped a strand of hair off my forehead. "You know what happens to cheaters." His eyes smoldered.

"No way! I want to do that again. I had no idea I'd be able to run like that. What else can I do?" I sat up on an elbow, eager to learn more.

"Do you enjoy swimming?"

"Depends on if there are any sharks."

"Kristia, sharks cannot kill us."

"But they could hurt us," I pointed out. If my skin tingled every time Ull touched me, I didn't want to know what shark teeth would feel like.

"I will keep the mean old fish away from you, sweetheart." Ull teased. "Other than an unnecessary fear of sharks you like to swim?"

"I do."

"Well, I do not know if I mentioned this, but we can hold our breath for a very long time."

"Like how long?"

"About two hours. Our physical makeup is similar enough to humans that we do require air eventually, but our genetic components are so streamlined we need a lot less of it than mortals do. Just like you need less sleep now than you did as a mortal."

"That's been beneficial this week." I nudged his arm. "Stop smiling."

"Sorry."

"But I'm a lot hungrier than I ever was as a human. Why is that?"

"You are using a lot more energy than you ever have before."

"You're terrible." I swatted the back of his head and he laughed.

"Well, there is that. But I literally meant you are using more energy now that you are a god. Our heart runs an average of forty beats per minute higher than a human heart because our bodies perform so many additional tasks. Immortality takes a lot of energy, so your body requires a higher calorie intake to function efficiently."

"I've never noticed Inga eating as much as I have this week."

"Inga is sneaky." Ull shrugged. "She does not like to stand out any more than she already does, so she does the bulk of her eating away from humans. You will see—now that you are a goddess, she will start eating more in front of you, too. She can pack in more than Gunnar."

"Skinny little Inga?"

"Do not let her fool you. Inga is a lot sturdier than she looks. I am sure she has told you she can beat us in fencing."

"She may have mentioned it once or twice." Or fifty times.

I stared at the sea foam, losing myself in the rhythm of the waves lapping at the shore. Even the tiniest noise sounded so clear now, from the water pulling away from the shore, to the sand crackling under the weight of the ocean, to the tiny crabs scuttling across the beach. It was easy to get distracted. But when Ull placed his hand on the bare skin above my bikini bottom and rubbed a small pattern with his thumb, my attention snapped back to the god in front of me.

"Do you want to try out the coral reef? It is really quite beautiful, and you will not need a snorkel. Unless you are too scared . . ." Ull taunted me again.

"Bring it, Myhr. I'm still waiting for you to kiss my feet."

"There would be no competition, my sweet, inexperienced wife. I can hold my breath a full three hours." He patted my hand consolingly as he tossed his shirt onto the sand. "You will catch up eventually. I have much more practice than you."

"That's right, because you're ancient." He sure didn't look it. The sun glinted off his tanned chest, and his bare skin glistened with faint drops of sweat from our run. His impressive musculature was highlighted by the fact that he wore nothing more than cardinal colored swim trunks.

"I do not feel old today." Ull laughed. "Shall we?"

He jogged into the water and turned to me, looking every bit the god he was. Even if I weren't dying to try out my new abilities, I would have followed him absolutely anywhere.

I peeled off my cover-up and stepped into the water. "Lead the way."

Ull's face lit up like a kid on Christmas morning. He

was so adorable when he was happy.

"If you like snorkeling so much, why haven't you gone since we've been here?"

"I wanted to go with you. I have never had anyone to do these things with before."

"What things?"

"Any of this." He held out a hand.

"Running? Swimming? You must have done this with Gunnar and Inga."

"When we were younger, I suppose we did. But it was never for fun. It was always part of some training regimen Thor dreamed up, or one of Inga's ridiculous challenges to prove she was as strong as we were." He shook his head. "Like we would ever doubt her."

Suddenly it hit me. Ull's childhood had been full of so many adult experiences. He'd never gotten to be a kid. He'd lost his dad, learned he was going to die, struggled to fit in to a new family with a seriously scary stepfather, spent most of his time with Olaug instead of Sif, and worried that his mom might disappear in battle just like his father had. This was the first time in his life he'd ever gotten to . . . to . . .

"Ull." I reached out and touched his massive bicep. It took everything I had to retain my train of thought. "You've never played before, have you?"

Ull shrugged. "Not particularly."

"And you're really enjoying this, aren't you?"

"You have no idea how much."

"Then enough talking. Let's go." I splashed him in the   face.

"You should not have done that, sweetheart. Now

I have to get you back." He stalked slowly toward me, a naughty twinkle in his eyes.

"Only if you can catch me." I splashed him again and dove under the water before he could get me back. I squeezed my eyes shut as I started in the direction of the coral reef, thinking the saltwater would burn. But after a moment I chanced a peek. I was surprised to discover the water felt no different to my eyes than air. If anything, my vision was even clearer beneath the waves, and I stared at the passing fish as my arms made determined strokes through the surf. I'd never swam in the ocean before; the waters of Northern Oregon, even in the summer, were far too cold for a lightweight like me. I expected it to be much choppier, but the reef seemed to keep the waves at bay.

When I sensed Ull approaching from behind I doubled my efforts, kicking as fast as I could. It was a nice surprise to find my legs were more powerful than I'd thought. I quickly outpaced Ull. My arms pushed the waves behind me stroke by stroke, and before I knew it I'd reached the reef. My human body would have taken three times as long to make the trip, if I'd been able to swim that far at all.

A hand grabbed my calf, stopping me just before I could touch the coral. I turned my head to find Ull waggling a finger at me underwater. I shot him an innocent look and he released my leg, letting me float to the surface. We popped up together, laughing.

"And how do you propose I get you back?"

"I can think of a few ways." I tipped my head back

41

and wiped the hair from my eyes. "But I believe you promised me a tour of the coral reef."

"I did, but . . ." Ull swam closer, and wrapped an arm around my waist. The teensy blue bikini I wore wasn't going to provide much protection from an amorous god. "What kind of warrior would I be if I let you get in two attacks without retribution?"

"Um . . ." I bit my lip. "A very, very sweet one?"

"Not my style, sweetheart." Ull treaded water effortlessly. I wrapped my legs around his hips and tried to sink him. "Nice try. But I am so very much stronger than you."

"For now." I kissed his nose. "I'm still new at this, remember?"

"I know." Ull lowered his mouth to mine and pulled me closer. Now we were skin to skin in the warm water. I rested my palm against his chest, feeling his quickened heartbeat beneath my hand. He let out a low moan, the vibration reverberating through his torso. The sensations were overwhelming, even to my newly-enhanced brain. I pulled back breathlessly.

"Is your idea of getting me back giving me a heart attack?" I teased, slowly unwrapping my legs so I could tread water of my own accord.

"Hardly." Ull's breathing was uneven, too. "We can head inside if you prefer."

"Ull." I laughed. "You promised to show me the coral reef!"

"Is that really what you want to do right now?"

"Um." I thought for a moment. "Yes. It is."

"As you wish, Mrs. Myhr." Ull dove beneath the water, surfacing thirty feet from where he'd been. "You coming?" The impish twinkle was back.

I swam after him. It was amazing to see Ull so carefree. He'd laughed more in the past week than in the nine months I'd known him. He paddled effortlessly along the surface as he waited for me to catch up, occasionally using his pointer finger to flick water in my general direction.

"Ull." I blocked the water with one arm in mock complaint. "I'm coming."

"Not fast enough." He dove under the water and surfaced next to me. "Look." He pointed. A school of brightly-hued fish swam underneath, making their way through the jagged coral.

"They're so colorful."

"Part of that is the fish; they really are bolder in color in this part of the ocean. But part of it is your vision."

"Huh?"

"We can see significant distances in inclement conditions. And certain colors also appear more vivid." He gestured to the fish before glancing at my bikini. "Royal blue is one of them."

"This is incredible." I put my face in the water to get a closer look.

"The water is not murky, is it?" Ull asked when I came up.

"No," I said with surprise.

"Again some of that is the water—it is naturally quite clear here. But the rest is a defensive mechanism. Our warriors must be able to defend attacks from any realm, including those submerged in water. Asgardian vision has acclimated over the years."

"I didn't understand what you guys meant when you tried to explain this before. This is kind of amazing."

Ull looked like he was about to burst with excitement. "You like it?"

"I love it."

"Dive with me."

I took a deep breath and followed him beneath the surface. His smile was contagious. He grabbed my hand and led me fifteen feet down, holding me steady as he pointed to his right. A turtle slowly made its way along the reef. Its leathery skin contrasted with the smooth shell, and its eyes were half closed, as if it were dozing. After an eternity it swam in front of us, taking no notice of the two tourists enjoying the view. We stayed where we were for a long time, watching an undersea scene I'd only ever experienced through nature shows. Being this close to this many fish was unreal.

I pointed to the surface, wondering when we'd need to head up for air. Ull shook his head. Guess he'd be more familiar with our limits than me. Ull tugged at my hand and we swam toward another grouping of fish. Equally as bright as the first, these were a luminous shade of orange that popped against the pink of the coral. They scattered as we approached, and I felt a little guilty for scaring them off. Ull turned to give me a warning glance. He held up one hand.

Stay calm, he mouthed. What did that mean?

Ull pointed ten feet below and I expelled half of the air remaining in my lungs with a silent scream. A small shark with black-tipped fins meandered through the reef. Fish disappeared into hidden coral caverns, and the turtle was nowhere to be seen. The shark seemed oblivious to us as it lazed through the water, but between my bulging eyeballs and the death grip I exerted on Ull's hand, he finally gave in to my panic. With an unnecessary eye roll, he pointed to the surface. I nodded frantically. His shoulders shook with unheard laughter as he pulled me up, though I needed no further invitation. Kicking as forcefully as I could, I reached the surface and paddled with frenzied determination for the beach. I would have run across the water if I could, but I had to settle for an almost cartoon-like motion of arms slapping waves until my feet touched the sand. My breath came in jagged gasps as I ran-swam for the shore with the desperation of a drenched cat.

I was clawing my way onto the sand with all the grace I'd had in my human life when I heard Ull surface some twenty yards away. The raucous laughter tipped me off.

"That was not funny." I panted, turning only when I was fully out of the water. I sat on the wet sand and hugged my knees to my chest, rocking back and forth.

"It was," Ull roared. He made slow strokes toward the beach and emerged from the ocean with considerably more dignity than I'd done. "It was a baby shark." His hooting began anew.

"Exactly. And who do you think was watching out for that baby? Its enormous, starving mother, that's who. I could feel her hungry, beady eyes waiting for me."

"Kristia." Ull couldn't stop himself as he gave in to a fresh wave of hilarity. "Reef sharks do not live with their mothers. They fend for themselves from birth. And even if they did have parental bodyguards, they could not hurt you. You are immortal, remember?"

"Immortal doesn't mean we're immune to pain."

"True. But I would not have let it come to that. And even if it did, somehow, get close enough to nip at you, you would have been all right. Your skin is impenetrable to shark teeth."

"Would have been a good discussion to have before you took me swimming with sharks," I muttered.

"I told you sharks could not hurt you."

"But you didn't say the impenetrable-skin thing." Ull's eyes crinkled and I could see he was about to give in to another bout of amusement at my expense.

I held up a finger to silence him. "Don't."

"Oh, come on, even you have to admit that was pretty funny."

"When I have calmed from my brush with death, I will consider said admission."

"Sweetheart." Ull scooted closer and slung an arm around me. Drops of water fell from his hair and glistened on his shoulders. How could anyone be so darned good looking?

"I'm mad at you for risking my safety."

"Darling." He brushed my forehead with his lips, still trembling with silent laughter. "I apologize. But I would never put you at risk. You have to know that."

"No more sharks." I held his gaze.

"Fair enough." His eyes still twinkled but it was the best concession I was going to get. "Now, how about lunch? Let me make it up to you with food."

"What did you have planned?"

"I was thinking shark fin soup." He winked.

"Ull!"

"Okay, okay." He chuckled as I shoved him toward the water. "Jerk chicken salads it is."

"Much better," I muttered as he scooped me into his arms, laughing all the way to the house.

CHAPTER FOUR

TRUE TO HIS WORD, Ull did not drag me into shark-infested waters again. We spent a lot of time walking on the beach of the Cay, picnicking at the edge of the water, and swimming in the late afternoon sun—*after* Ull did a careful scope of the water for sharp-toothed infidels. I took advantage of my husband's inability to play board games to beat him soundly in round after round of wholesome family fun. By all accounts, it was the perfect honeymoon.

Until the dream.

"Again, my babies." An oversized, gnarled figure crooked her finger at three tiny creatures. Once more I was struck by the feeling that I was somewhere in the past, though I couldn't place the era. My vision was obscured in patches, so I couldn't make out the tiny forms with any degree of clarity. They appeared as blurred orbs, almost as if someone had scrubbed them from my vision with a blunt eraser.

I was able to see the mottled giantess. She was in what seemed to be an outdoor courtyard. The grass within the walled enclosure looked freshly mowed, and a cardboard box sat at the giantess' feet. A horde of rats squirmed inside the box, climbing on top of each other in a desperate attempt to break free of their prison. The giantess placed a single rat on the grass, and pointed to one of the blurs. "Your turn."

The orb moved toward the rat, emitting the unnerving sounds I associated with horror movies. I hadn't watched many; I was more into period pieces and the occasional chick flick. But the snarl coming from the orb was enough to set my teeth on edge. Although I couldn't make out definitive movements, my vision allowed me to see the blur barrelling toward the rat. The animal hissed, then scurried across the lawn. It tried to climb back into its box, but the orb sent a rock flying, knocking the rat back onto the grass. The orb snarled again, and leapt toward the rat. The rodent fell onto its back, limbs bent in rigor mortis. The blur had killed it.

"Very nice," the giantess praised. "Now, make room for your brother."

A second orb approached the box, and the giantess lifted a rat onto the grass. It shot a glance at its dead compatriot and took off across the lawn. The second orb slunk through the grass with determined speed. It quickly overtook the animal and covered it with its own body. I couldn't see through the blur of its shadow, but if the sounds coming from its victim were any indication the rodent was being asphyxiated. Quickly.

My stomach lunged as a shiver wracked my spine.

"Your turn, daughter. Do what you do best."

The third orb moved for the box. Her mother set her prey on the grass, and watched with a cruel smile. The orb let out a shriek and the rat ran. The orb flickered and disappeared, reappearing directly in the rodent's path. It clawed at the orb, then turned in the opposite direction. The orb flickered and reappeared again. The rat bared its teeth, striking to defend itself. With a shriek, the orb began to vibrate. It sent a pulse of white light at the animal that left it suspended in mid-air. With one final hiss, the orb pulled the energy back. Her victim fell to the ground, dead.

"Well played, all of you. And to think, you are only toddlers. The gods will be grossly unprepared for the three of you when you come of age." The giantess looked at her charges lovingly. "Now, go inside and wash up. We wouldn't want to be late for supper."

My hands shook as I watched the family leave the courtyard. Those things were vicious—and they were toddlers? What would they be like in a few years? Was there any way we could hope to survive them?

"Sweetheart?" Ull's hand was cool against my forehead. "Are you having a bad dream?"

"Mmm?" I dragged my eyes open and glanced at the clock. It said we'd been out for ten hours, but I felt like I'd barely slept a wink.

"You are hot. And you were tossing. Are you feeling all right?"

"I think so." I tried to pull the last few minutes from my subconscious, but I couldn't remember a thing. If I hadn't been dreaming, why did I have this overwhelming sense of dread? And the uncomfortable feeling of being unprepared?

"Perhaps you are hungry," Ull offered.

I pushed myself up on my elbows. "Maybe."

"Let me make us some breakfast." He swung his long legs off the edge of the bed and picked his shirt up from the floor. He began to pull it over his head, but I stopped him with a hand on his back.

"Leave it off," I whispered. "I like the view."

Ull tossed the shirt back on the floor. "I aim to please." Then he sauntered toward the kitchen with a wink over his shoulder.

I flung myself back on the bed and tried to figure out why I felt so out of sorts. The word *unprepared* kept coursing through my head. I had no idea what it meant, but I had the sinking feeling I'd done enough relaxing for one honeymoon. It was time to put my warrior-husband to work.

❄ ❄ ❄ ❄

I knew Ull wasn't too excited about showing me how to fight, but I also had a nagging feeling I didn't have much time left to learn *a lot* about self defense. I decided to broach the subject that afternoon, and I decided to broach it very carefully.

"Wow, sweetheart." Ull lowered his aviator shades, and gave me a rakish grin from his beachside chaise. "To what do I owe this honor?"

"Just wanted to bring my darling husband a cold beverage." I batted my eyes as I handed him the icy glass. I hoped I'd mixed it right—I'd never made a mojito before.

"In your tiniest bikini?" He raised an eyebrow at the barely-there white number Victoria had tucked away in my suitcase. I'd been horrified when I discovered it, but from the look in Ull's eyes, it had the desired effect.

"Get over here." Ull set his drink down in the sand and patted the lounge chair. His bronzed chest glistened with drops of seawater from his afternoon swim, and his black shorts clung to the muscles in his legs. I sighed. He was just so beautiful.

He moved a fraction of an inch to the side and I tilted my head. "There's no room."

"Exactly." He tugged my arm, pulling me down on top of him. My hands landed firmly on his pecs, and I ran my thumb over the taut surface. I felt him shiver.

"Do not start what you cannot finish, Mrs. Myhr."

"Oh, I can finish." I ran my finger to the center of his chest and drew a line up his sternum to his neck. My legs tangled up in his, and I rubbed my toes along his calf. He raised one eyebrow and placed one hand firmly on my behind.

"Well, then. By all means." He squeezed and my face flushed.

"Ull!"

"I told you not to start."

"Actually, I had a better idea." I traced the outline of his lips with my finger.

"Seriously, Kristia? You can think of something 'better' to do?"

"Okay, not better. But . . . different?" I kissed the

corner of his mouth.

"I like different." Ull's eyes rolled back into his head as I bit at his bottom lip.

"Well," I continued, squirming on top of him until his eyes popped back open.

"Darling, if there is something else you would rather be doing I suggest you spit it out. Otherwise I am taking you back to the house immediately."

"All right." I kissed his upper lip and propped myself up on my forearms. My hips pressed into his and he closed his eyes again.

"Kristia!"

"Okay. I just thought, since it's just you and me out here . . . that maybe . . . you could show me one of your moves?"

"Oh, I will show you some moves all right—"

"Ull!" I reached back to pull his hand off my bottom. "That's not what I mean. Teach me just one teensy little thing I could use in a fight. Just for fun. Please?"

Ull's eyes closed beneath his sunglasses and a small *V* formed between his brows. "Now?"

"Please," I pleaded, kissing a small trail from his neck down his chest. "I really want to learn. I'll do anything you want if you just show me a few little things."

"Anything?"

"Anything." I kissed down to his belly button, where the saltwater pooled in the small rivet. Ull groaned.

"All right. But it is going to cost you dearly." He

propped himself up on his elbows.

"I'm willing to pay. Now show me." I scooted back on his legs so I sat up on my heels.

"What do you want to know?" Ull lowered his sunglasses lazily and eyed me with a look that made my insides burn.

"Well." I paused. "Uh , . . What am I supposed to do if I'm attacked?"

"You mean if this happened?" Ull launched himself off the chaise, wrapping one arm around my waist and dragging me across the beach. He cradled me in his arms and landed in the froth where the ocean met the shore.

"See? I'm totally defenseless." I gazed up at him, my back pressed firmly against the wet sand. He hovered, supporting his weight on his forearms.

"I am afraid you are." Piercing blue eyes locked in on mine. Between the depth of his stare and the heat from his abs, I forgot everything else.

"Um . . ." I bit my bottom lip.

Ull tilted his head to one side, a small smile playing on his mouth. "Now what did you want to know?"

"I—"

A wave washed over us. The warm saltwater lapped up to my waist then retreated, leaving a film of sand over my legs.

"You were asking me how to defend yourself?" Dangit, it was hard to focus with Ull's dripping body pressed against mine. Yes, I wanted whatever it was I'd asked about. Self-defense. Right. But there was something else I wanted more.

I bent my knee and twined my calf around Ull's. I shifted my hips just an inch and stared into those endless eyes. They sparkled in the sunlight. My arms were trapped beneath his torso, so I turned my palms upward to touch the spot where his chest met his shoulders. It was so smooth, so firm, and so very, very warm.

My eyes never left his as I moved my thumb along the line of his shoulder, over his bicep, and down to the crook of his arm. I drew a slow circle inside his elbow and Ull blinked.

"Kristia," he whispered.

"Yes?" I tried to reach up to stroke the stubble lining his square chin, but my arms were pinned.

"You are not trying to defend yourself."

"So?" I raised my head and kissed his jaw. "Maybe I don't feel like fighting you off."

"Mmm." Ull closed his eyes as I kissed my way up to his ear. "So if someone came after you, you would just let them do this?"

He swiftly rolled onto his back, forcing me on top of him. He shoved his fingers in my hair and tugged gently, pulling my head back. He kept the other hand just above the bottom of my bikini, firmly pressing my hips into his. I squirmed against the hold, trying to find a way out of his grip. Though I tactically had the upper hand, I couldn't move.

"Well, I wouldn't let just *anyone* do this."

"I should hope not," he growled softly. He raked his teeth along my throat and paused at the hollow of my neck. "Because if I ever caught wind of someone

55

doing this to my girl, it would end very badly for them." He ran his tongue along my collarbone. I shivered.

In a lightning-quick move, Ull flipped me onto my back and pinned my arms above my head with one hand. I gazed adoringly at the fierce assassin glowering over me. "And this. What would you do if someone did this to you?"

"Uh." I blinked. If I told Ull what I really wanted to do right now, I'd turn every possible shade of crimson.

"Focus, Kristia." Ull stared at me. "What would you do if you were trapped?"

"I . . . uh . . . I'd . . ." My cheeks felt hotter than a grizzly in a desert. "You seriously want me to fight you off?"

"If you are so bent on going through with this little exercise, then yes. Give it your best shot. And then, I believe, you promised to pay me for the lesson."

"Gladly." I narrowed my eyes and wrenched my arm as hard as I could. It didn't budge. I tried again but it was futile.

"You are outmaneuvered and I am twice your weight. Try something else," Ull commanded.

I threw my shoulder into his chest and tried to roll to one side.

"You cannot out-force me. Look at the difference in our masses. Think tactically, Kristia. What can you do that will debilitate me?"

My eyes widened. "You don't want me to—"

"I want you to find a way to get me off you. Do what you have to do."

I closed my eyes and raised a knee to his groin. Ull groaned and rolled off me.

"I'm so sorry! You said to—"

He raised a hand and waved at me, turning away.

"I'm sorry," I repeated.

"That was good." He rolled back with a grimace. "But if someone is bent on capturing you, they will come back for more. And quickly. Your next step should be to run."

"If you want I can get some ice for—"

"Run, darling." It was a threat. "Now."

I jumped to my feet and took off down the beach. I ran just shy of the shoreline, where I was less likely to be slowed down by soft sand. The water lapped at my heels as I built up speed, pushing off the balls of my feet. A warm breeze caressed my bare skin and every cell in my body buzzed as if someone had turned on a light switch. Movement came so easily now.

Something hot hit me from behind, and I felt Ull's arms curl protectively around me as he tackled me to the ground. We landed just inside the surf again, and this time the wave crashed over our heads. I sputtered as the water covered my face, wishing I'd had time to hold my breath. The saltwater burned my nose.

"You did not run fast enough, sweetheart." Ull was on top of me again, and this time he wasn't hovering. The full weight of his body pressed me into the sand. His legs were tangled up in mine, and his hands cradled the back of my head.

"I thought I did a pretty decent job," I objected.

"And yet here we are. Again." He brought his teeth

57

to my throat and bit gently, making my insides churn. I threw my arm around his back and tried to wrench him off me, but he didn't budge.

"Out-massed, remember darling?" He swirled a slow circle at the hollow of my neck with his tongue.

"I'm not kneeing you again. I want to *enjoy* my honeymoon, you know."

I felt Ull's smile against my neck. "Then think of something else."

"I don't want to hurt you." I protested.

"You are the one who wanted to learn defense. So far we know you are not a fast runner and you have a mean left knee. That is not enough to help you in real combat."

There was nothing that ruffled my feathers like a challenge. "Fine."

I dug my fingernails into the flesh on his lower back and scratched a trail from his spine to his hip. He winced.

"That is a start. But for maximum impact dig your thumb here." He covered my hand with his and placed my thumb just above his hipbone. "Angle your finger downward and jab."

"I don't want to hurt you—"

"Do it, Kristia."

I dug my thumb beneath his bone and he doubled over. "That is good," he groaned.

"I'm so sorry—"

"Stop being sorry. If push comes to shove, you are right: I want you to defend yourself. Now stand up. We need to work on your speed. I cannot have my wife being outrun by every dark elf in Svartalfheim."

CHAPTER FIVE

BY THE END OF the day I'd nearly doubled my running speed. Ull kept his promise and made sure I could deflect a handful of common attacks, though he insisted that I'd never need to use any of it. He would protect me. Or my bodyguard would.

Visions of my imminent jailer danced in my head and I shoved them to the side. At least for now, Ull and I were completely and totally alone.

I relished every minute of it. Every night at dusk Ull would take me out to the beach. He'd made it his mission to teach me to dance. He worked his way through the old Norse folk dances, and then showed me steps that would have made Fred Astaire proud. One night we waltzed under the stars and the next we practiced the tango. I had to draw the line at the foxtrot—no sense pushing my coordination's luck, though it was showing no sign of slowing down. And when Ull whipped out the Teton Mountain Stomp, I doubled over laughing.

"What is that?" I hooted.

"One of *your* folk dances."

"We did that in fifth-grade gym class. I am *not* square dancing on my honeymoon." I clutched my sides.

"Suit yourself. I was just trying to honor your heritage."

"How about we do the awkward American junior high sway-and-turn?" I stopped laughing and pulled him close, resting my head on his chest. He wrapped his arms around my waist and pressed his hand into the small of my back. I stared at moon reflecting off the ocean, bathing the beach in a soft glow, and I sighed contentedly.

"Sounds perfect. Or . . ." Ull paused. He moved his hands over my bottom and gave a gentle squeeze.

"Or?" Boy, howdy, I liked where this was going.

"Or I could show you how to make it snow."

"Is that some kinky Asgardian phrase for something else?"

Ull let out a deep, guttural laugh that rang along the beach. "Well, it is now. But I meant it literally. Do you want me to show you how to make it snow?" Ull kept one hand firmly on my bottom and raised the other in front of his face. He waggled his fingers at me. "These things are magic."

"Oh, I know they are." I twirled a lock of his hair around my pinky. "Especially that thing you did this morning, when you—"

"That is not what I meant." Ull did his best to look

stern, but a grin broke across his face before he could stop himself. "You did seem to enjoy that."

My eyebrows shot skyward. "Enjoy seems a bit of an understatement, considering that you could have heard my—"

"Do you want to learn the snow thing or not? Because I am having a change of heart." Ull squeezed my backside again as his eyes glazed into an inky blue.

"Um . . ." I bit my lip. "How about you show me real fast, and then we can go with your Plan B."

"Excellent." Ull stepped back and held out one hand so his palm faced the sky. He took a breath and the inkiness drained from his eyes. "Sorry, sweetheart. This takes a lot of concentration, and it is easier if I do not touch that." He nodded to my tush.

My insides warmed. "Fair enough."

"We gave this a go back at the church. You did well enough—"

"I killed a squirrel," I whispered. It had been mortifying. Right after our wedding, Ull had tried to teach me to channel my inner winter, and I'd ended up standing in my wedding gown in the middle of a courtyard, cocooning a squirrel in a sheet of ice.

"You did not kill the squirrel. You just . . . delayed its journey."

"Because you unfroze it. Poor squirrel." I closed my eyes.

"No matter. You understand the fundamentals: center yourself in the portion of your head that felt most affected when Odin activated your immortality. Channel the weather pattern you wish to affect, and draw it to the tips of your fingers. Like this." Ull closed his eyes. He inhaled slowly and brought his fingertips together. After a moment he opened his eyes and lifted his hand, digits still touching. When his arm was at eye level, he opened his palm. A filmy fog circled in his hand. He blew gently and the fog raised four feet overhead. Ull turned his palm down, pointed at the swirl, and drew his hand back. The fog morphed into a thick cloud, and a layer of snow began to fall. It melted when it hit the ground, the moisture turning the moonlit sand from silver to dark tan.

I shook my head. "I can't do that."

"Yes you can." Ull nodded at me. "Close your eyes. And draw your energy to that spot inside your brain."

Hoping Ull didn't see me cringe, I probed my brain for the spot Asgard's Goddess of Wisdom and resident neurosurgeon had drilled with her ridiculously large needle. It was easy enough to find—it was the spot that felt like it had been battered with a searing-hot branding iron, then pummeled with a meat cleaver. My wedding day hadn't been all sunshine and roses. But Ull didn't need to know the extent of what I'd had to go through to become like him; it would only upset him. Besides, any pain I'd gone through had been more than worth it.

I'd gotten Ull.

"Are you centered?"

I took a moment. "Now I am."

"Good. Picture whatever kind of weather you want to affect: snow, ice, hail, rain . . . whatever suits your mood. When you are ready, send that impulse out to your fingertips."

I squeezed my eyes harder and moved the snow cloud through my body until my fingers felt cold. "I'm there."

"Now open your eyes and blow the impulse into the air."

After slowly exhaling I opened my eyes. A fluffy white cloud hovered in my palm. It looked exactly like the one I'd pictured, and for a moment I was so surprised, the cloud flickered in and out of focus.

"Do not lose your connection to it," Ull cautioned. "If you allow yourself to be distracted it will disappear."

"I'm trying. I just didn't think it would actually be there."

"You underestimate yourself, Kristia. You are capable of more than you know." Ull crossed behind me. Now his breath was cool on my neck, and his hands were again cupping my behind.

"Thank you. But that is not helping me focus." I nodded to the cloud, which was now practically transparent.

"Right. Sorry." Ull stepped back. "Now let it go."

I stared at my palm and brought my lips together in a loose O. With a gentle breath I pushed the cloud up until it hovered a few feet away. "Now what do I do?"

"Now you activate it." Ull gestured with his finger and I copied the movement. A flurry of thick, white flakes fell from the cloud, melting on the sand next to Ull's significantly prettier ones.

"My snowflakes look like drowned cotton balls." It was hard not to sound dejected.

"But you made snowflakes," Ull pointed out. "It is not easy to learn this skill, and you produced precipitation on your first attempt."

"I nearly killed a squirrel on my first attempt," I corrected. "This is take two."

"Regardless, you have done well." Ull clapped his hands together once, and our clouds disappeared. "Would you like to try again? Maybe something like this?" He took a breath, then sent a beam of ice onto the sand. He waved his hand in a circle until a small frozen pond appeared. "Fancy an ice skate?"

"Uh, no. Not the best idea for me." Even with my newly enhanced agility, ice-skating would be pushing my luck. One did not simply forget nineteen years of sheer and utter lack of grace; not even when one became Goddess of Winter.

"Care to make a pond, then? Or are you scared of that too?" Ull crossed his arms.

He knew me so well. "Oh, it's on." I closed my eyes and drew all the cold I could muster to the tender spot in my brain. Then I pushed it to my fingertips. They felt cooler this time, almost uncomfortable. The feeling built until I couldn't take it anymore, and I pushed my hand away from my body. "Ouch!"

My eyes flew open as sheets of ice shot from my fingertips. They coated the sand in a thick blanket, creating a frozen surface that was a tenth of the size of Ull's. When the ice stopped flowing, I cupped my hand to my chest, rubbing to stop the burn.

"Darling." Ull stepped in and raised my hand to his lips. He sucked each finger in turn, rolling his tongue across the pads until the pain was replaced by a much more pleasant sensation. "You did well."

"Um . . ." My eyes rolled closed as Ull kissed my palm. "Was it supposed to hurt?"

"It has been a long time since I learned this skill, but I remember it being uncomfortable the first few times, *ja*. It will get easier with practice." He sucked gently on the inside of my wrist. "Would you like to try again?"

I opened my eyes and watched his lips move against my skin. "Um . . . yes?"

Ull looked up from his ministrations with a raised brow. "Am I distracting you?"

"You know you are." I pulled my arm away from his mouth and pointed a few feet away. "Maybe you'd better stand over there."

"Whatever you like, darling." Ull stepped aside and folded his arms. "Try the snow again. And ground yourself. The more firmly you are rooted to the earth, the easier it will be to channel the elements."

"Easy as that, huh?" I closed my eyes and focused. This time when the cloud left my palm, it emitted thick, fluffy flakes. And once the sand was covered in fresh snow, my palm felt cool, but the burning sensation was gone.

"Very good Kristia," Ull praised. "Again?"

I nodded and repeated the motions, this sending a tiny blizzard that dusted the shore from Ull's feet to the water's edge.

"Well done." Ull ran a hand through his hair. "Are you ready to retire for the evening?"

"Not quite. I want to try the ice thing again first."

"Ah." Ull crossed to my side and wrapped his arms around my waist. "As you saw, ice can be tricky. Try drawing your power from here." He placed one hand on my stomach, just below my belly button. I shivered.

"Okay."

"Now close your eyes," Ull instructed. "Center your mind. And pull from this." He pressed gently against my skin, and I jumped. A frozen stream flew from my palm to the sand, creating a tiny sheet of ice on contact.

"Woah," I murmured.

"Mmm." Ull rubbed his nose along the back of my neck. "Not bad. Care to try again?"

"Okay. But it's kind of hard to focus when you're doing that."

"Right." Ull stepped to the side and crossed his arms again. "I will behave. Go."

Ignoring the insanely beautiful deity staring me down, I closed my eyes and focused on the spot in the middle of my brain. Then I pulled all the power I could manage from my center, and released the energy through my palm. When I opened my eyes, the tiny sheet of ice had grown to the size of a tennis court. It was nearly as big as the one Ull created.

"Kristia Myhr." Ull slow-clapped his approval from two feet away. "I am impressed."

"I kind of am too," I admitted. "I was afraid I was going to freeze a crab or a seagull or something."

"You underestimate yourself." Ull closed the distance between us and peppered a trail of feather-light kisses along my forearm. Where my skin had been cool just moments before, it suddenly felt like it was about to combust. "Now may we go inside to celebrate?" Ull used the tip of his tongue to draw a small circle on the inside of my elbow. My knees buckled, and he caught me in his arms.

"Mmm, yes please."

"Your wish is my command." Ull marched toward the house with determined strides. Now that his mouth wasn't touching my flesh, my head began to clear. There was so much I still needed to learn if I was going to be of any use come Ragnarok. Maybe we shouldn't be spending so much time . . . honeymooning. Maybe I was being selfish.

"Ull," I ventured, hesitant to break the mood.

"Yes." Ull didn't stop walking. We were ten feet from the porch steps.

"Would you be up to another training session tomorrow? With weapons, maybe?"

The *V* between Ull's brows popped and he skidded to a stop. "You ask this now?"

"I'm just worried. I've only just learned the weather thing. And I don't know a whole lot about how to defend myself," I hedged.

"You are doing fine. Your hand-to-hand training was more than sufficient. Besides, I thought we agreed that I would look after you."

"We did. But you know me. Luck favors the prepared, right?"

Ull stared at the house. The French doors leading to the bedroom were mere feet away. "You are anxious."

"A little," I admitted. "I just feel like there's some piece I'm missing, and when it finally comes together I'm afraid it'll be too late."

"Too late for what?" Ull rubbed his thumbs against my hips.

"I don't know. That's what's bothering me. And until I figure it out, I want to make sure I'm doing everything I can to take care of our family."

"It is not your job to take care of them." Ull looked me square in the eye. "They will take care of you. You are brand new to all of this. Nobody is expecting you to jump in with both feet."

"I am," I countered. "It's what I've done my whole life. I don't go halfway on anything. It would make me feel better if I had at least one weapons lesson under my belt. Please?" I wrapped my arms around his neck and blinked up at him. Then I shifted in his arms so my bottom pressed lightly against his hips.

"Holy Helheim, Kristia. That is not fair."

I pressed harder.

"Kristia!"

"Will you do it?" I asked.

Ull let out a low growl. "You know I will."

"Thank you." With a smile, I rested my cheek against his chest. His heart thudded steadily against my ear.

"One lesson. That is it. But you know it is going to cost you."

Ull lifted me so I could wrap my legs around his waist. Then he dropped his head to my neck and made a series of bites that sent heat spiraling down my torso. My eyes rolled closed as the bites moved lower. When they reached the neckline of the dress Victoria had designed, I dug my fingernails into his neck. Ull ran his nose along the edge of the fabric, letting out a slow breath that made my skin feel like it had been raked with an electric prod. Every nerve ending was almost uncomfortably alert.

Ull slowly dragged his nose back and forth along the fabric until he came to rest at the low dip of the V-neck. He kissed the swollen flesh, then lifted his head to meet my hooded eyes. "You willing to pay, Mrs. Myhr?"

My nails grazed the top of Ull's back, drawing small circles along his spine. "Name your price."

Ull broke into a slow grin. His eyes moved from the French doors to the sand. "*Faen*," he swore. "I am not going to make it." He lowered me onto the sand with one hand, and ripped his shirt off with the other. Then he moved over me, so I could feel the heat coming off his chest in waves. *Hot bejeebus . . .*

He chuckled. "Name your price, eh?"

"Anything," I breathed.

"Why, Kristia." He blew softly in my ear and I shivered. "I was hoping you would say just that . . ."

CHAPTER SIX

"**KRISTIA? WILL YOU PLEASE** come down here?"

Early morning light streamed through the kitchen window as I stood at the counter, stirring sugar into my tea. After I set my spoon in the sink, I turned toward the sound of Ull's voice. The living area was empty, so my eyes moved outward to the verandah. No Ull.

"Where are you?" I called back.

"Down here." Ull sounded far away. I eyed my tea wistfully.

"I'm coming." With a sigh, I picked up my oversized mug, cradled it in both hands and padded across the cool wooden floor. My silk nightie and matching robe didn't provide much protection against the light breeze wafting through the open windows, but since they'd been such a hit the night before I hadn't wanted to change.

Actually, it was entirely possible I was going to

stay in this outfit for the rest of my existence.

"Where are you? Wait, did you say 'down here'? This is a one-story house." My head whipped around as I tried to figure out where Ull might be.

"No, it is not." Ull's head popped around the doorframe of the walk-in closet in the living area. "Come with me."

"Into a closet? Is this some weird Asgardian version of Seven Minutes in Heaven?" I shrugged. "Okay. I'll play."

Ull's eyes moved from my grin down my torso, stopping at the hem of my robe. It didn't cover much—in fact, it stopped just below my tush. He stared at the expanse of bare skin, and when he finally opened his mouth he spoke to my legs. "I thought you wanted to learn weaponry. But think I like your idea more."

I was *so* happy I'd let Victoria pack my honeymoon wardrobe.

"You're actually going to teach me to fight with weapons?" I squealed.

"I promised I would." Ull's eyes didn't leave my legs. "Lucky for me, I am a very efficient teacher. I believe we can wrap this up by lunchtime."

"Perfect. But if we're not playing a junior high kissing game, why do you want me in a closet?"

"Because this is not a closet." Ull smirked.

I sighed. "Of course it's not."

"Follow me." Ull held out his hand. I shifted my mug to one hand and twined my fingers through Ull's as he stepped into the tiny space. Ull held his thumb to a small picture on the wall. It emitted a series of beeps, then retracted.

"What the . . ."

Ull lowered his face to the hole as an optical scanner emerged. The white beam ran along his eyeball while I tried not to gape. Satisfied with its reading, the beam disappeared and the entire wall dropped, revealing a spiral staircase. Ull squeezed my hand and pulled me after him, down the steps and into a massive room.

"Of course. You've got a secret hidey-hole here too." It was official. The surprises would never end.

"Not as comfortable as Ýdalir's, but it will do for a vacation residence." We followed the stairs down to the second story, glowing wall sconces lighting our path. Once we reached the lower floor Ull tapped a panel and the lights brightened, illuminating the couches, table, and large open space.

"Where's the kitchenette? What if I want some tea while I'm picking out my . . ." I crossed the dark wooden floor to the glass case on the wall, pausing to touch the soft leather of the couch. This was such a man-cave. My eyes landed on a metal ball covered in spikes. "Is that a mace?"

"Indeed." Ull came up from behind and wrapped his arms around my waist. He rubbed the silky fabric of my robe against my stomach, and I nearly dropped my mug. "And do not worry about the missing kitchenette. If you want more tea, I will be happy to run upstairs and fetch it for you."

"I love that about you." I turned in his arms and kissed him. Hard. Then I pulled back and beamed up at him.

"We could always do this later. Maybe in an hour?" He ran his palms down my thighs, sending a wave of goose bumps across the exposed skin. I took a determined step back and cupped his cheek in my palm.

"For that, I'm going to need more than an hour," I murmured.

"*Faen*, Kristia. You kill me."

"You're immortal. You'll survive."

Shaking his head, Ull crossed to the glass case. He rested his palm against a flat metal surface on the wall, and it beeped. The glass slid to the side.

"Pick your poison."

"This is . . . wow." I joined Ull at the case and ran my fingers across the flat surface of a shiny, metal blade. It was three inches thick and easily as long as my torso. The thing looked like it weighed a ton. To its right was a star-shaped blade hung from a leather rope, and on its left was a thick wooden club with curved blades sticking out of each end. "I don't even know what half of them are. Can you really teach me how to use them?"

"Eventually, yes. Some of them are fairly easy to pick up, like this one." Ull pointed to the long blade. "Broadsword is a matter of speed and strength. It is one of my favorite weapons. Others are slightly more strategic, like this." He touched a longer, thinner blade with an elaborate handle. "This is a rapier. It is Inga's favorite. Because of it's relatively light weight, the angle and force of the impact determine the extent of the damage to its victim. Then there are these." He gestured to a series of smaller weapons that looked more like torture devices. "These require direct application to an attacker, which means you would need to be sufficiently skilled to debilitate them hand-to-hand. You will get there, but it will take some time."

"So what should start with?" My vision swam at the wall-to-wall weapons case. Even with eternity stretching in front of me, I wasn't sure I'd be able to learn to use them all.

"Good question. You are petite, so the mace would not work well for you. You are a novice, so nunchucks are out. You have decent speed and an impressive strike, so the dagger could work. But I think you might be best suited to this, actually." Ull carefully removed a shiny silver sword and offered it to me. Its slightly curved blade was longer than my arm, and it had a thick handle wrapped in black leather.

"There are two." I nodded to the sword's slightly smaller twin, still in the case.

"I know. How about we start with the one and work our way up?"

"You're the boss." I shrugged.

"About time you admitted it." Ull winked. "Now this is a katana. And yes, they can be used with a mate. You hold it with the edge facing away from you, like this." Ull wrapped his hands around mine, placing the hilt of the sword in my palm. It was lighter than it looked, maybe two or three pounds. I lifted it experimentally. "Feels nice, eh?"

"Yeah," I admitted.

"For now, use both hands on the handle—right on top, left an inch beneath. Try to keep your thumbs and forefingers a bit loose, to maximize movement of the sword. Remember if you are gripping it too tightly, you might not be able to strike as quickly as you need. And with this weapon, range of motion matters."

"Got it." Ull guided my hands back and forth experimentally. Since he was wearing black pajama bottoms and no shirt, I couldn't help but lean into his bare chest. He smelled incredible; his woodsy scent mixed with the beachy air to create an intoxicating cocktail that left me breathless.

"Pay attention, Kristia," Ull admonished.

I forced myself away from the planks that were his pecs and gripped the sword. "Yes, sir."

"Now, it is important to deliver a clean cut with the katana. Because of the curvature of the blade, it is easy to misdirect your strike. But remember, a ninety-degree slice is going to have a much deeper impact on a target than being struck with the broad end of the sword. *Ja?*"

I nodded, then I removed one hand from the hilt and touched the edge of the blade. It was sharper than any knife I'd ever owned. Anyone on the receiving end of this wouldn't be feeling too great the next day . . . if they were feeling at all.

"Shall we go outside and practice?" Ull took the katana from my hands, and grabbed another curved sword from the case. One corner of my mouth turned up.

"I thought you'd never ask."

I followed Ull up the secret stairs, through the living room and onto the beach. My eyes watered when we stepped into the bright sun, but I exhaled and blinked back the tears. I was getting a handle on my new sensitivities, but occasionally the effort required more focus than I was able to muster. Things like light and heat were more easily controlled. Ull's touch was still an entirely different matter.

I glanced down as Ull led me across the sand, and I sucked in a breath. I was still wearing what I'd worn to bed. Hardly fitting combat attire. I turned on one heel and headed back to the house.

"Where are you going?" Ull's hand on my arm stopped my trajectory.

"To change. I forgot I was in . . . well, this." I gestured to the barely-there nightie and robe.

"I did not forget." Ull's eyes shifted to the inky blue I'd come to love.

"Ull." I palmed his chest. "I can't learn how to fight you wearing this. Even if it weren't wildly inappropriate, my sleeves are too billowy. They'll get caught on the blade."

Ull dropped the swords and tugged the sash off my robe. In one swift movement the flimsy fabric was pooled at my feet, and I stood on the beach in nothing more than a black negligee.

"Ull!"

"Problem solved. Weapon up." He handed me a sword with a sexy grin, and walked toward the edge of the water. Then he bent in a low crouch and held his blade at chest level.

"Seriously? We're just going to go for it? In . . . this?" I gestured to my outfit. I looked utterly absurd.

"You afraid?"

"No," I huffed. I stormed down the beach and copied Ull's pose. "Now what do I do?"

"Now you defend yourself." Ull crossed to me. He swung his sword in a circle above his head and brought it down just above mine.

"Hey!" I held up my sword to block him, and jumped back. "That wasn't fair!"

"All is fair in love and war. And this is quarter speed. Our enemies will not go so easily on you."

Well that stunk worse than a week-old fish fry.

"All right. Go again."

Ull repeated the same move and I blocked him. Again and again he swung at my head, every strike picking up speed until the blade was nothing more than a blur. Each time I stopped it with my own weapon, but I felt the reverberations through my forearms. It should have made me tired, but instead I felt invigorated; I was finally learning something that could tangibly help protect us.

After I blocked my fiftieth blow, I put my hand on Ull's arm. "Can we switch?"

"Of course." He grinned. He dropped his sword and closed the distance between us. He wrapped both hands around mine and pressed against me from behind. His bare chest was damp on my back. I tried my hardest not to picture the drops of sweat trailing along his impossibly perfect abs.

I failed.

"Swing like this." Ull moved my sword over my head in a slow circle and then brought it down in a line perpendicular to my body. As he moved, he pressed his hips into my bottom. The fabric of my nightie rose another half-inch.

"Like that, huh?" I repeated the swing, this time exaggerating the movement in my waist.

Ull groaned. "Keep that up and I am taking you inside."

"Oh, you could take me *out*side." I grinned. "But not now. It's my turn to whomp on you for a while."

Ull raised one eyebrow. "Do not get cocky, Mrs. Myhr."

I turned to blink up at him. "It's not cocky if it's true." I shoved him toward his sword and he chuckled.

"I like this side of you."

"And I like that side of you." I eyed his spectacular behind as he bent to pick up the katana. He turned with a raised eyebrow, and my eyes dropped to his bare chest. "That side, too."

"One more comment and swordplay is done. Now, strike."

"Yes, sir." I gripped my hilt lightly and swung the sword. It bounced off Ull's with a little too much force.

"Very good, Kristia."

"You don't have to sound surprised," I grumbled.

"Now do it again, a little slower this time, and draw your power from your legs. Then I want you to drive your sword directly into the sand, as if you were staking it. You might not always have a blade at your disposal, but if you find yourself in a dire situation, and you are able to locate any sharp object—a rock, a stick, a branch with a severed edge, if you can get one—if you use that object to bear down directly on your attacker, then you might be able to debilitate him, at least long enough to run away."

"I don't run away," I reminded Ull.

"One day you may have to. Now strike."

I did as instructed, repeating the moves until I could do them to Ull's satisfaction. Then we moved on to side strikes, jabs, and footwork.

After two hours, Ull wiped his brow. "How about a little game?"

I shook out my arms. The muscles had stopped burning half an hour ago; now they just felt numb. Apparently supernatural goddess strength was no match for two hours of Ull's unrelenting training. "What did you have in mind?"

"One round. Winner has to make dinner."

"Fair enough." I crossed in front of Ull and drew my sword. "Get ready to get cooking."

Ull narrowed his eyes. "Pretty confident there."

I tossed my hair over my shoulder. "Oh, it's on."

I lunged for Ull's chest but he blocked my jab. He swung his sword in one hand, driving it at my side. I jumped back. Then I swiped my blade in a diagonal arc, forcing Ull to step to the side. With his footing off-balance, I swung again, nicking the skin on his forearm. Crimson liquid bubbled at the surface, and dripped onto the pale sand. I threw my sword down and ran to his side.

"Oh my gosh, I'm so sorry! I hurt you!" I put my

fingers on the wound to stop the bleeding. When I pulled them away, the blood was gone. "What the—"

"Sweetheart. Our skin heals almost instantly. Do you really think I would swing this thing at you if I could hurt you?" He held up his sword with a raised brow.

"Oh. I didn't realize . . ."

"But now that I have you here . . ." Ull's eyes shifted to my favorite shade. He wrapped his arm around mine, pinning me against his chest. Then he lifted his sword to my shoulder with a lazy smile. "Checkmate," he breathed against my ear.

"What? No. That is not fair."

"It is perfectly fair. You disarmed yourself. You came running to me. If you ask me, this is an all-out surrender." Ull flicked his sword and it sliced the thin strap of my negligee. My hands flew to my chest just in time to stop the silky fabric from falling. Ull's chest vibrated against my back as he chuckled. "You want me to do the other one or do you admit defeat?"

My breath hitched as Ull ran his nose along the side of my neck. "I want a rematch," I demanded. Only it came out as more of a question.

"Oh, do you?" Ull raked the bottom of my earlobe with his teeth. "Well I am the winner. And I want something else."

He dropped his sword and clotheslined me behind the knees. In one swift move I was cradled in his arms, his mouth crushed against mine. My fingers wrapped around sweat-streaked strands of blond hair, pulling him closer. Ull's tongue probed the front of my teeth and I parted my lips to let him in. He tasted like pine, and mint, and sweat, and I sighed as his tongue massaged mine. When he pulled back to suck on my neck, my eyes rolled back in my head.

"You always get what you want, don't you?"

"No." Ull didn't look up from his ministrations. "But I will spend the rest of my existence making sure that *you* do."

With characteristic determination, Ull held me to his chest and ran for the house. And for the rest of the morning, he stayed very, very true to his word.

CHAPTER SEVEN

DESPITE MY EXHAUSTION, OR maybe because of it, I'd slept like a hibernating bear since we arrived on Asgard Cay. I had no memory of slipping into the dream, but one minute I was wrapped safely in the arms of the God of Winter; the next I was in an ornately-decorated hall somewhere far from my happy place.

The air felt cool against my bare arms, the silent chamber thick with the quiet of a sleepless night. Not even a cricket stirred outside the oversized windows. It was unnatural. Something about the room made me feel like I was in an earlier era, though I had no way of knowing for sure. A breeze blew against my legs and I glanced down with a groan. Apparently I'd decided a lacy, blue nightie made for appropriate travel clothes.

Fabulous.

My knees gave out beneath me as a furious roar rang through the space. I dropped to the ground, scraping my thighs on the rough stone floor. Heavy footsteps thundered outside the room, and I scrambled on my knees to dive on the far side of an enormous cupboard. My shoulder struck a basket of blankets someone had placed against the wall, and I threw one over myself to avoid being seen. Then I lifted the blanket just enough to peek out. I kept my face to the ground and poked my head around the corner of the cupboard. As I watched, the door burst open, and two figures stormed through. They were shrouded in shadows, their faces obscured by traveling cloaks, but as I peeked around the corner of the cupboard, I could make out the difference in their size. The first appeared to be a male of human stature, a little over six feet tall. He moved with an air of grace as he swept through the room. The figure behind him seemed to be a female over twice his height. She moved with the refinement of an inebriated mountain goat. She stormed behind the man, emitting a grating wail I could have sworn I'd heard before. Twice, she tripped on the benches strewn throughout the hall. When she stumbled a third time, she picked up the offending furniture and threw it at the wall behind me. It ricocheted off the cupboard, splintering into a thousand pieces and showering shards of wood across my back. One pierced the blanket and dug into my flesh like a tiny needle, making me wish I'd worn my thick flannel pajamas to bed. The extra coverage, though unflattering, would have come in handy.

"Where did you take them?" the woman shrieked. "Where are my babies?"

The man turned on one heel, his hands steepled

*together. When he spoke, his voice came on a hiss.
"Patience, Angrboða."*

*The enormous woman swiped at the man and he
dove out of her reach, landing unceremoniously on the
floor. The female stormed to his side. "Where are they?"*

*The man righted himself. In the moment he pushed
his hood slightly off his face, I caught a glimpse of
something familiar, but before I could register what it
was, he tugged the hood over his jaw, so he was
completely obscured.*

*"Angrboða." The man shook his head. "Have you no
faith? The children are with their father. He will take
care of them."*

*"That's not possible. They can't be with you—you're
here." The woman raised her hand and the man stepped
back.*

*"Oh, am I?" The man waved his arms in front of him
and his figure disappeared. A voice came from the spot
where he'd been standing. "Or am I just a projection?"
He flickered back into view.*

*"You sent a hologram to tell me you took our
children? You selfish, evil . . ." The woman lunged and
her hood flew off her face. For the first time I could see
her grotesque features: yellowed, pointy teeth set
against purple lips. Dirty, mottled skin covered in pox,
and stringy, blue hair that fell to her waist. From what I
could remember from Olaug's lessons, she seemed to be
a mountain giant. Her people loathed the gods, to the
point where they'd staged a dozen rebellions in the last
five hundred years. Two had nearly been successful.*

"Ah, ah, ah." The man wagged his finger. "If you hurt

85

me again I won't tell you where I've sent them."

"You have one minute," the giantess hissed.

"Do you remember their prophecy?"

"Of course. The three of them together will bring an end to Asgard." Recognition dawned on the giantess' face. "Have you sent them to fulfill their fates?"

"Indeed." The man crossed his arms, his voice dripping with satisfaction. "They are safe with me, inside Asgard's walls."

"The gods will be dead by morning." Angrboða clapped her hands together. The joyful gesture was a contrast to her dour form.

"Not so fast. First they must turn themselves in."

"But the prophecy said—"

"The prophecy said they would end Asgard. And they will. But to do so, Odin must believe he has them under control. He has hunted them all these years— once he believes they are no longer a threat, he will let his guard down and they can do their jobs. The children are aware of this. And they are prepared." The man walked to the window and faced outside.

"Will they be hurt?"

"No more than necessary. The girl will be given a realm to rule. Odin will unknowingly hand her an entire army to assist our cause. The boys will be separated, one cast to Midgard, the other guarded in Asgard. But when the time comes, they will break their entrapments. And they will be ready."

The giantess' eyes glazed, and I saw the ember of excitement begin to glow. "So it begins," she whispered with a crooked smile.

"So it begins," the man confirmed.

The room filled with an air of evil, a sick joy passing between the cloaked figures. I drew my knees to my chest and curled up against the side of the cupboard. Then I pulled myself out of the vision, willing myself back to my happy place. I tunneled through the blackness with enough force to propel a rocket. My overwhelming anxiety filled me with a sense of dread. Whatever the monsters had been plotting, it hadn't sounded good for my family.

I dragged my eyelids open and turned toward a familiar smell. Tears streamed down my cheeks, and I buried my face into the taut muscles in front of me. Ull woke with a start, pulling me close and brushing his lips against the top of my head.

"Sweetheart. It is okay. Everything is going to be okay."

"No, it's not!" I wailed. "They're in Asgard! Or they were. Or they're going to be. I don't know what I saw. Or even when it happened. But it'll be terrible. And I didn't stop it!"

"Shh," Ull soothed. He stroked my hair while I cried myself out. My tears came in heaving sobs, the undignified kind one should never emit in front of others. But Ull didn't judge me. He cradled me between the ridges of his biceps while my eyes poured and my nose ran all over his impeccably perfect torso. When the muscles between my ribs hurt too much to cry anymore, my wails gave way to whimpers. Eventually I felt numb.

"Oh, Kristia." Ull reached with one arm to tuck a

sheet around me. "You are freezing."

"I'm f . . . f . . . fine."

"Your teeth are chattering. Here." Ull lifted my chin with his forefinger. He pressed his lips gently to mine, holding perfectly still while I struggled to do the same. "Oh, sweetheart." Ull squeezed me gently, the thick muscles of his arms wrapping around the thin fabric of my nightie. I felt so safe pinned to him, the heat of his body coursing against my skin. It wasn't long before my jaw stilled and my breathing slowed to match Ull's rhythmic heartbeat. When a full minute passed, Ull pulled his head back. Then he brushed two fingers against my temple. "You look like you have seen a ghost. What happened in that head of yours?"

"I have no idea," I admitted. "One minute I was here, and the next I was in some . . ." My brain fought against itself. It felt like something was blocking the path to my vision. I tried to push around the obstruction, wanting to remember every trivial detail of my time in that disturbing dream. But the only things I could remember were the feelings—fear; desolation; anger; and finally, joy. None of it made any sense.

"Where were you?" Ull pressed.

"I can't remember," I admitted. "It was a big room, I think. But I don't remember what it looked like, or what was outside the windows, or even why I was there. But I remember a conversation. Something terrible was planted in Asgard. And whatever it was, it'll be the end of everything." I tried to bury my head against Ull's shoulder, but he held my chin lightly

88

between two fingers.

"Try to remember. Did it feel like the past? Present? Do you remember who was in the room with you? You said something was going to be the end of everything. What do you mean?"

My head moved back and forth. "I don't know," I whispered. "I just know that something awful is about to happen. I wish I could remember more." Tears pooled in my eyes. Ull wiped them with the pad of his thumb before they could overflow.

"This is twice in two weeks that you have not been able to remember your visions. It worries me."

"I'm the worst goddess ever! I have one job, and I'm failing miserably." The tears began anew.

"Shh. That is not what I meant. You are doing just fine. Someone has figured a way to block your visions. Whether the person you are seeing is wiping things clean from inside the vision, or someone from the outside is telekinetically tampering with your memories. I do not know."

"Gods can do that?" I sucked in a breath. The sudden rush of air chilled my teeth.

"Some gods can," Ull confirmed. "Which means other races could have the ability as well."

"How would that work? Both scenarios."

"Let us assume this is a tenth realm vision. You have left your physical body to travel to the spirit plane."

"It can't be." I shook my head. "If that were the case, I'd bring my visions back with me." Most people were taught that the mythological Norse universe contained nine realms, when in reality there were ten. That tenth realm existed solely to acquire information—a spirit could leave its body and travel to the realm, procure whatever information it needed, and bring it back to its physical form. It could be dangerous to separate spirit from body, but I'd never heard of a situation in which you didn't bring your memories back with you . . . unless you didn't make it back at all.

"Not necessarily. The location you visited could have a device called a block. That block would prevent you from carrying any memories you created while on the property back to your physical self. So if, say, you happened to visit the same location in both of these visions you cannot recall, then I would assume that whoever resides at that location would have placed a block somewhere within the property. That would mean anyone attempting to project their spirit onto the property would be unable to recall what they had seen once they returned to their home realm."

I rubbed my eyes. "There's a technology to keep you from bringing knowledge back from the tenth realm?"

"Yes. I have never seen it, and to my knowledge no one I know has ever encountered it. But I do believe it exists." Ull stroked my cheek with his thumb.

"And the other scenario—the mind-altering thing. That's terrifying."

"I know." Ull's mouth turned down. "But I do not believe that is happening to you. If it were, you would display symptoms throughout the day, not just after two isolated visions."

"Thank heavens." I exhaled. The idea of someone getting inside my head was almost as disturbing as knowing something horrible was coming to Asgard. "But how am I supposed to protect everyone if I can't remember what I'm seeing?"

"It was only two instances," Ull mused. "I am willing to wager you visited the same location both times, and that location has a block somewhere on site. If that is the case, it will not affect what you see anywhere else."

"But what if the bad guys know that? If they've figured out there's one secret meeting spot they can go to, and we'll be none the wiser because it's a blind spot for the newbie goddess?"

"I have news for you," Ull whispered in my ear. "The bad guys are not that smart. In thousands of years, Asgard has never come close to falling, in part because of our highly organized military, and in part because our enemies are extremely simple beings. Whoever placed this device would have to be paranoid for an all-together different reason. Who knows? It could even be an overprotective parent trying to shield her children." Ull chuckled. "Inga's dad has done far worse to keep her safe."

I mulled over Ull's assessment, his words triggering something. It was fuzzy, and I couldn't put my finger on what it was, but the tickle in my mind confirmed he was on the right track.

"That feels right, I just don't know what it means yet. So what do I do?"

"Exactly what you are doing." Ull ran his nose along my neck, and I shivered. "Share your visions with me as you have them. Let me help you with your physical abilities, so you feel you have the tools to defend yourself if need be." Ull blew lightly into the hollow of my neck, then traced a small circle with his tongue. "And if you are truly concerned, feel free to let me help take your mind off things."

Ull raked his teeth across my collarbone, and my eyes rolled closed. Then he laced his fingers through mine, running his free hand down my arm. The backs of his hand transferred an almost unbearable amount of heat to my over-sensitive skin, and when he reached my shoulder he continued down along my ribcage, before placing his hand firmly around my hip. He jerked me against him. The sudden increase in pressure made me gasp. My body responded instinctively. But I took a deep breath. Before things could go any farther, there was one more thing we needed to discuss.

"I really hate to say this, but I think we should go home soon."

"Anything you want, my love." Ull nipped at my ear and I groaned. "Are you not enjoying yourself here?"

"I've never been happier in my entire life."

"Then why would you want to leave?" Ull's tongue dipped just behind my earlobe. Good gravy. It took everything I had to retain cohesive speech.

"Because . . . um . . . oh. Right." The forgotten vision. "Because I think something is coming for us. Can't you feel it?"

Ull raised one blond eyebrow. "There is only one thing I feel right now. Want to hazard a guess as to what it might be?"

"I'm nervous, Ull. If whatever I saw tonight was right, then sooner or later things are going to head south. And when they do, I don't want to be thousands of miles away from everyone we love."

Ull eyed me levelly. "You amaze me, Kristia. We are on our honeymoon, and you have the perspective to think about our family."

"How could I not?" I blinked. "I love them."

Ull kissed my forehead. "Fair enough. When would you like to leave?"

"I don't know. A few days, maybe?"

Ull threw his leg over my hips and rolled on top of me. He wrapped long fingers around my wrists and held my hands over my head, pinning me down. I squirmed, but he held on tight; I couldn't get away.

And I didn't want to.

He stared down at me with inky eyes, and all the blood drained from my head. My insides began to buzz as Ull lowered his face to whisper in my ear. His breath was cool as he spoke, and icicles traced an intricate pattern as they skated down my spine.

"Well then, darling, we had better make the most of those last few days. Starting with tonight."

When I shivered, Ull let out a low groan. He pushed his tongue against my lips and I parted them to let him in. He licked lightly at the tops of my teeth before pushing deeper. My free hand flew to his hair, fisting the sleep-tousled strands and pulling him even closer. We'd talked enough.

I shifted so our foreheads were touching, then I opened my eyes and blinked up at him. He stared back at me, his eyes my absolute favorite shade. With a grateful sigh I pulled his face to mine, murmuring my promise against his pale, pink lips.

"You don't have to ask me twice."

❄ ❄ ❄ ❄

My hands flew to my stomach as I awoke with a start. It had been five days since we'd talked about leaving, but neither of us had been able to tear ourselves away. Since we'd landed on Asgard Cay it was like time had stopped, and nothing else existed. Maybe it was the magic of the island, or maybe it was the fact that we could finally be alone together, but whatever it was, we'd been so wrapped up in each other we hadn't paid attention to anything outside this little bubble.

Now the spell was broken.

"Do you feel that?" I rolled over and rested my chin on Ull's bare chest. It rose and fell rhythmically, but I could tell his breathing was forced. The pounding of his heart against my jaw betrayed his fear.

"Yes," he whispered. His gaze was locked on the ceiling.

"I feel like the world just dropped out from under me. What does it mean?"

Ull's eyes found mine. The anxiety in his stare took me back. Ull was the epitome of confidence, even in the most terrifying situation. But whatever woke us up must have been worse than I imagined.

"Oh my gosh." Tears pricked at the corners of my eyes. "What does it mean?"

Ull shook his head, forcing his features into a neutral position. "I am sure everything is fine, sweetheart. Maybe we ate some bad beef."

"That's not true, and you know it." I blinked back the tears. "What's happening?"

Ull rubbed his hand along the small of my back. It felt warm against the fabric of my negligee. "I honestly do not know. But I think we need to pack."

Ull wrapped strong arms around me and kissed the top of my head. My chin quivered. "I guess the honeymoon's over."

"Impossible." Ull stilled my chin with a kiss. "This was only the beginning."

I nodded, and rolled out of his arms. "I'll get the suitcases."

"I will call the Valkyries," Ull countered. He picked up his phone from the nightstand and dialed. "Give me a status report." He barked into the device. He listened for half a minute, then shook his head. "There has to be something more. Kristia and I both felt a shift. Have you checked with Tyr? I understand he has returned to Asgard." After another moment of silence, he nodded. "*Ja*. I understand. Bring the plane around immediately. How quickly can you have it here?" He looked at me and held up two fingers. "Two hours will do. See you then."

He put down the phone and stood facing the open French doors. He wore only striped pajama pants, and his bare back was tensed against the light morning

95

breeze. Each individual muscle was bunched into a tight knot, matching the fists he held at his sides. With the light reflecting from the ocean outside, and the glow hovering just above his tousled blond strands, he looked more like a god than ever.

"How about I make us breakfast while you throw everything in the trunks?" he offered. "I have a feeling we are in for a long day."

"Oh, Ull." I crossed the room in bare feet. The scrap of fabric I'd worn to bed barely covered my bottom, and I snuggled against Ull for warmth. His arms felt so safe; for a moment I felt like if I just stayed here, in his arms, in this room, on this island . . . then maybe everything would be okay. That whatever monsters were chasing us would go away once and for all. But I knew life wasn't that simple. Bad things happened. Bad things *were happening*. And we couldn't just hide away forever, not when everything was on the line.

"Nothing went down." Ull stared at the ocean.

"Really?" I followed his gaze. "Then how do you explain that feeling right here?" I pressed my palm against the ridges of his abdomen. God, he was strong. I pressed again, running my thumb lightly along the crevices between the muscles. The blood started to drain from my head as I stared at the ripples, and without realizing what I was doing I kissed the bicep pinning me in place.

"I do not know." Ull was unresponsive to my advances, a sure sign there was something amiss. "But I have a feeling we are going to find out soon enough." With a sigh he squeezed me to him, then relinquished

96

his hold. "Omelets okay?" he asked as he crossed to the door.

"They're perfect." My voice was barely a whisper. Ull was so spectacularly beautiful, both inside and out. It had been such a blessing to watch him let his guard down, to see him truly relax for the first time since we'd met. But now the wall was back up. Duty called, and I had no idea how long it would be before Ull would let his carefree side come out again. "Hey," I called as Ull stepped out of the bedroom. He turned, a thin T-shirt halfway over his head. "We'll always have the Cay, right?"

Ull gave me a tight smile, then pulled his T-shirt down as he strode toward the kitchen. I stared at his back as he tore ingredients from the fridge, willing the moisture to stay in my eyes. I couldn't ignore the pit in my gut that told me things were about to get ugly.

And from the way Ull was butchering onions on the chopping block, I knew his gut told him the same thing.

❄ ❄ ❄ ❄

My sleep on the flight home was disturbed. I drifted off with surprising ease, but my mind immediately filled with dark images—the snake and the wolf that were mainstays of my nightmares; a sea of dark, deserted buildings shrouded by big, black skies. I didn't have much control over what I saw, and I was glad when the darkness cleared and gave way to a beautiful apple grove filled with laughing friends. Instinctively I knew it was Asgard, and I watched as Thor, Sif, and a group of equally beautiful gods stood in a circle.

"Throw it, Sif, throw it!" A brunette goddess clapped her hands. My sightline came over Sif's shoulder to see a familiar face standing in the center of the circle with his arms spread open. His kindly facial features were lit up in a huge smile.

"Come now, Sif," Balder spoke. "You know what my mother said: she had every being in the realm take an oath to protect me. Even the Norns cannot challenge that."

He motioned for Sif to throw her rock and she did. It hurled at Balder's chest, veering off course at the last possible moment. The group cheered.

"I told you." Balder laughed.

"Now me." A short god holding a bow and arrow stepped forward. "It's only mistletoe."

"The most harmless thing in all the realms. Take your best shot, brother!" Balder waved him ahead.

"No! Wait! Do not shoot!" A raven-haired woman dove for the arrow. She was seconds too late.

The scene shifted into slow motion. The shorter god drew his arrow, and the sprig of mistletoe ruffled at its end. Balder put his arms in the air in mock surrender, laughing the whole time. The arrow left the bow, traveling at half-speed toward its target. But at the last moment, where it was supposed to veer off course, it shot straight through Balder's left wrist. The shorter god's face dropped in horror. Balder clutched at his arm in confusion. "But Mother said . . ." He pulled the quiver out with great effort, watching the red liquid drip down his palm.

"Balder! No!" The dark-haired woman ran to her son. "Mistletoe is so small; I didn't ask it to protect you. And it struck your hjerte vene—your heart vein is . . . is . . ." Her eyes spilled over as she clutched her son. "This is all my fault!"

Balder dropped to his knees and his mother fell with him. Blood covered them both, flowing more freely as Balder pulled his hand from the wound.

"Brother." The shorter god stepped forward. "I am sorry. I had no idea. He gave me the arrow." He gestured toward the forest, where I saw a cloaked figure lurking in the shadows. When I squinted, I was pretty sure I could see Elf Man hiding under that hood.

"Who?"

But Elf Man was gone. The gods gathered around Balder in horror. He had grown unnaturally pale.

"My son. No!" The woman sobbed in earnest. Sif sniffed delicately, turning into Thor for comfort. All of the gods began to weep as Balder dropped fully to the ground, and took his last breath.

Ragnarok had begun.

CHAPTER EIGHT

"ULL, WAKE UP. WAKE up!" I shook my husband, who had fallen asleep holding me on one of the jet's extra-wide lounges. He rolled his head to the side but he was out like a hibernating bear. "Wake up! Now!" I thumped his chest with my palms until he opened one eye.

"What is it?" He tried to pull me closer, but for once I wasn't in the mood.

"Balder is dead."

That did it. Ull sat up so fast he nearly threw me off the chair.

"What? When? Did you have a vision?" He reached out to grab me just in time, catching my waist before I could topple over.

"I don't know when it happened, but in my vision everyone was standing around, throwing things at him because he thought he was invincible. I guess his mom did something?"

"She made everything in Asgard take an oath not to hurt him," Ull murmured. "What did she miss?"

"Mistletoe. And the elf who has been coming after me in my dreams gave this shorter god an arrow laced with mistletoe and he shot it and . . ." I didn't want to say any more.

"And Balder is gone." Ull finished for me. He closed his eyes. "Oh, Kristia. Do you realize what this means?"

I nodded. "Ragnarok has started. It's inevitable now, isn't it?"

"Yes." Ull kept his eyes closed. He pulled me to him and buried his face in my hair. "Darling, are you certain you want to go through with this? I can take you to one of the safe houses until all of this is over. We can go back to Asgard Cay, or to the house in Alfheim, or—"

"Ull Myhr, how dare you think so little of me? Our family is not going to face this without me. I'm the only one the Norns haven't seen coming, remember? I'm the only shot we have at surviving this thing. And I was *not* raised to turn my back on the people I love when they need me."

"But your bodyguard is not scheduled to begin until next week. You cannot put yourself at risk until I know I can protect you. I shall contact Thor at once to arrange—"

"We have bigger problems. I'm going to do what I can to help."

"I am still not comfortable with this."

"Neither am I," I answered honestly. "Not entirely. But it has to happen. Otherwise we both lose the people we care about. And I can't allow that—not when there's something I can do."

Ull grabbed my hand. His trembling fingers betrayed the fear he held back from his voice. "We will call Olaug when we land. I am certain Odin has sent instructions for us."

❄ ❄ ❄ ❄

Odin did have instructions: we were to spend the night in London, get as much rest as we could, and head to Ýdalir first thing in the morning. Olaug would brief us from there.

It wasn't the best night's sleep I'd ever had. As I tossed and turned, my too-familiar nightmare visited me again. Now my images were much more vivid.

Ull and I stood in the field of lavender, hands clasped to meet our destiny. This time we were surrounded by our family: Sif, fierce in her armor; Thor, Mjölnir clasped firmly in hand; Odin, his great robes billowing in the howling wind; Gunnar and Inga, battle swords drawn at the ready; and Olaug, heartbreakingly frail yet resolute in her desire to protect our home. The wolf and the snake stalked toward us, angry beams shooting from their eyes. As we stood together, awaiting the approaching onslaught, the angry beams turned to sparks and the field burst into flames. The animals pulled back, their mission accomplished. Closer and closer the fire lapped toward us, determined to envelope us in its angry death. But just as it reached the spot where we stood the sky opened up, a great dark hole taking its place. The hole grew larger and larger, opening like a vortex and bearing down on us with the ferocity of a tornado, plunging my nightmare to blackness.

Strong arms held me tight as I bucked against the vision. My shoulders wrenched back and forth as I fought to pull myself out of the dream. I kicked my legs, and let out a shriek so loud a dog on the street began to bark. Only when I realized I was safely ensconced in Ull's arms, lying in the king-sized bed of our Kensington row house, did the terror start to subside. It gave way to heartbreak as Ull whispered into my ear.

"Shh. Darling, it will be okay."

"Maybe," I whispered back.

"Why do you say that? I vowed to protect you, and I have never broken a promise."

My fingers stroked the stubble along Ull's jaw. "I know you'll do everything you can. But I don't know if I'll be strong enough to fight this. It's too powerful."

"Do you want me to take you back to the Cay? It is protected. Nobody will be able to find us there."

"You know I can't do that." My eyes pleaded with Ull. "I'm not walking away from our family. Ever."

One corner of Ull's mouth turned in a sad smile. "How can the thing I love most about you be the very thing that drives me mad?"

I let out a sound that was half laugh, half sob. "I just feel like I haven't prepared enough. I'm afraid that when it's time for me to see whatever it is I'm supposed to see, I'm going to let you all down."

Ull's eyes softened. His lips brushed my forehead, and he squeezed me against his bare chest. "You could never let me down. How about I tell you another story?"

"That's really sweet, but I don't think a bedtime story's going to help. Warm milk isn't going to do much here, either."

"I think you might want to hear this story."

I lifted my head. Ull was smirking at me.

"Go ahead." I rested my cheek on his shoulder while he drew tiny circles on my hip with his thumb. If he was trying to distract me, he was doing a bang-up job.

"A long time ago there was a very young warrior. He was fresh out of the academy, and he thought he knew everything about combat."

"Was this warrior a devastatingly handsome blond?" I teased.

"Perhaps." I could hear the smile in Ull's voice. "Okay, so I was fresh out of the academy and I was arrogant. I was assigned command of a unit, and we were charged with disabling a minefield the mountain giants had set just outside the Dark Forest. It was a rookie job, and I thought I was too good for it. I stormed into HQ and demanded a serious combat assignment. The commander stared me down. 'Son,' he said. 'This *is* a serious combat assignment. You do not disable those bombs, and a lot of gods are going to die.' He dismissed me with an inane hand flick, and went back to his paperwork.

"I was furious. The two years I had spent studying hand to hand, weapons, tactical, every program the academy had for specialist assassin training: it all seemed like a joke now that I was being sent to do a Level One forensic job."

"Disabling a minefield doesn't seem like an entry level test," I interrupted.

"In Asgard, it is. Believe me, we have far bigger threats lurking in our shadows than explosives."

I shivered.

"Needless to say, I stormed out of the commander's office and took it out on my troops. My orders were halfhearted and ill thought-out, and I sent them into the field without adequately briefing them on the realities of the situation. The mountain giants had set twenty bombs laced with poison, some rigged to launch at fifty yards, and my men had no way to see them coming."

"Oh my God," I whispered.

"Thankfully, none of them were hurt. Even without proper briefing, they assessed the threats, eliminated them strategically, and completed the mission without issue. Well, mostly without issue."

I cringed. "What happened?"

"I was so in my own head, I missed an obvious trap. I stepped right onto a hotspot, and triggered a detonation. It should have blown my head clean off, but Gunnar saw the device and acted fast. He pushed me into the forest just as the bomb went off; he took a heavy hit to his arm, saving my sorry back. I would be dead if he had not acted—and it would have been my own doing."

I let out a slow breath. "I'm glad you were both okay."

"Back then I was egotistical, overconfident in my abilities, to the point where I lost sight of the real threat. A lot has changed since then. But I want you to hear this so you will understand how very ready you are for whatever it is that lies ahead of you."

My hair tumbled against my shoulders as I shook my head. "I'm anything but ready. I barely know how to separate my spirit from my body, much less what I'm supposed to look for once I do."

"But that is just it. You know how much you do not yet know. Your humility combined with your willingness to put in the work, are the very qualities that will force you to succeed. The fact that you wanted to spend our honeymoon learning to fight; that even after months of studying, you worry you will not know what to do when the moment comes; that diligence proves that you have the tools to get through this.

"Ull," I whispered.

"We never know when our time is going to be up. If Gunnar had not saved my life that day, I never would have come to Midgard. I never would have met you. I never would have known what it feels like to be truly happy, and I never would have let myself experience love." Ull held my chin between his pointer finger and his thumb. Then he pressed a soft kiss to my lips. "The point is, life, even an immortal life, is unpredictable; messy; heartbreaking; and at times, downright beautiful. All you can do is your best in any situation you are dealt. And then you have to trust that the people around you will have your back. You might not feel like you are ready to take on whatever it is the Fates have asked of you." He held my gaze. "But I know you. You are smart, determined, and one of the most driven individuals I have ever met. If I thought I could convince you to run away and let me keep you somewhere safe until all of this is over, then believe me, Kristia, I would try. But you do not operate that way. And I know you are not going to back down, no matter what I say. This is not going to be easy; we are fighting for Asgard's very existence. But I have every confidence that you will do exactly what you set your mind to." Ull's lips curved up. "I would hate to be Loki about now. He has no idea what is coming for him."

My eyes filled with tears as Ull rested his forehead against mine.

"*Tro*, love."

"What does that mean?" I wiped my cheek.

"It means faith. Sweetheart, when the only thing you have left is faith, just take my hand and believe."

"Oh, Ull." I threw my leg across his hip and rolled on top of him. "I love you."

"I love you more." His eyes twinkled at me. He cradled my cheeks with both hands and brought my face to his. His lips pressed lightly against mine in a sweet kiss. Then he gently shifted me so I was beside him, tucked securely under one arm. "We should try to get some rest. Tomorrow is going to be a long day."

"I know." I closed my eyes and willed myself to go back to sleep. But the effort was about as useful as a trapdoor on a canoe. And if the steady tapping of Ull's finger on his chest was any indication, I wasn't the only one with insomnia.

Neither of us got much sleep that night. Instead we lay in the darkness, trying not to think about the uncertainties the morning would bring. Soon enough we would be with Olaug and Elsker. If I did my job right, we would all be safe soon. It was time to master my abilities—fast.

❄ ❄ ❄ ❄

When we got to Bibury the next day, dusk was falling on the quiet country town. We made our way up the gravel drive, too somber to appreciate the familiar musicality of the trickling fountain. When we opened the door we were overcome with mouthwatering smells. We entered the kitchen to find Olaug pulling a roast out of the oven while an apple pie cooled on the counter. Her expression was grim.

"Eat," she instructed. "Ull, your father wants to see you when you finish your meal. Go downstairs and instruct Heimdall to open the Bifrost. Kristia, you are to stay with me."

Ull squeezed my hand and shot me an anxious glance.

"It is all right, Ull—I will protect her in your absence. I promise," Olaug finished. I nodded at him, realizing she was giving me the privacy I needed to focus on this, my greatest task. Saving Asgard.

"Fine. But do not get into trouble, either of you." Ull held out my chair and we sat down to eat. "Kristia, do not do anything brave. Just stay here with Olaug. No heroics. Agreed?"

Olaug caught my eye and gave a small nod. We

would have to tell Ull what he needed to hear or he would never leave for Asgard. I didn't want to worry him any more than absolutely necessary . . . and I wasn't entirely sure I'd be able to focus on finding the tenth realm with an anxious god hovering over me. I crossed my fingers underneath the table. What Ull didn't know wasn't going to hurt him. Besides, Olaug said she would protect me. How much trouble could we really get into? "Agreed."

We ate in earnest. We had a long night ahead of us.

But something was off. Olaug wasn't herself. She was normally a strong, vivacious woman, similar in many ways to my own grandmother. Tonight she was quieter, slower, and much wearier than I'd ever seen. Ull seemed too worried about me to pay attention to much else, so I didn't bother pointing out that Olaug seemed practically frail. But the moment we saw him safely through the Bifrost I pointed to the leather chair next to the armor with my sternest face.

"Sit," I commanded.

"Pardon?" Olaug tutted her disapproval. "Kristia, you know we do not have time for pleasantries."

"I don't care. Sit down while I fix you a cup of tea."

"We really cannot—"

"Please, Mormor," I pleaded. She softened at my nickname.

"Oh, all right. But we have five minutes. That is all."

"I only need four." I turned for the small kitchen in the chamber below Ýdalir and quickly assembled a pot of hot water with teabags, lemon, and honey.

Olaug tilted her head when I brought her the tray.

"Thank you, Kristia, but I prefer milk."

"I know you do. But if you're sick—and don't try to tell me you're feeling one hundred percent because it's obviously not true—then you need lemon and honey."

"Kristia." Olaug shook her head. "I am fine. Really."

"What's going on?" I knelt beside her and poured the tea. "Does it have anything to do with that dream I had the night before my wedding?"

"Your dream?"

"My *dream*." I waited, but Olaug just blinked at me. "You know, the one where that monster Elf Man said he gave you a magical disease? That it was going to . . . really hurt you. And the only way to heal you would be to destroy him?"

"I do not know what you are talking about."

"Stubborn Asgardians," I muttered as I squeezed lemon into her cup. "I'll get it out of you eventually. You may as well tell me so I'm not distracted for the rest of the night. You know I need to focus."

"Very well." Olaug took the teacup gratefully. "But I do not want you to tell Ull just yet. He worries enough about things."

Truer words had never been spoken. "What's going on with you?"

"I do not know." Olaug's forehead wrinkled as she furrowed her brow. "I have never felt ill a day in my life. Gods cannot be sick; you know this."

"I do."

"But these past few days have been so different. I feel like I have lost strength. It started two days ago.

110

When I woke up I was tired, and I am never tired when I wake. I have gone to sleep and gotten up at the same time for the past—well, for a long time."

"I'm sure." My own grandmother had been a creature of habit after seventy-two years. I could only imagine the kind of routines one could establish after an eternity.

"But I was exhausted from the minute I woke up. I would have gone back to bed if I weren't so confused. How can a god feel sick?"

"What happened?" I sat across from her and poured a cup of tea for myself.

"I went about my day as usual, but with each hour I felt weaker. It was like something was taking my strength from the inside. At first I could handle the physical rigors of the day: cooking, tidying, my calls to Asgard, but by early afternoon, I had to lie down. I slept through the rest of the night. And of course, by morning, I'd heard about Balder."

"Did you feel at all rested in the morning?"

"No. I felt worse. My bones ached and I was exhausted."

"Do you need apples? Do you want me to call Idunn?" Apples seemed to be the answer to everything around here. The goddess Idunn had developed a special hybrid to provide the gods with immortality. I'd have run to Asgard that moment if I'd thought it would help, but my gut said differently.

"She dropped off a fresh batch three days ago. I am fully stocked."

"Have you told anyone what you are feeling?"

"With all that is happening in Asgard, my body should be the furthest thing from anyone's mind."

"Don't say that Olaug. How could we not worry about you, especially now? That creep I've been dreaming about made it very clear that he was going to do everything he could to stop us from interfering with 'his plan,' and right now someone very evil is executing a very dark plot against our family. And Elfie gave you some magical disease. I think it's all related."

"I had not thought of it that way."

"If it's the same guy I've been seeing, the only way to get you better is to defeat him." I locked my jaw. "So help me, if he does anything to you we can't undo I'll knock him halfway to next Tuesday."

"Kristia. I am certain I will be fine."

"You will be. Because I am going to find his sorry hide and rip it limb from limb." Nobody was going to hurt my granny. Not if I had anything to say about it.

"Kristia." Olaug pursed her lips, but there was a smile in her cheeks.

"I mean it. I love you, and this is just not acceptable to me." I stood. "Are you well enough to work tonight? If you need to lie down . . ." I paused. What could we do? The fate of Asgard rested on our shoulders. If Olaug and I couldn't manage to locate whoever was doing this to us and identify their plan of attack, we'd have a lot more to worry about than Olaug's illness.

"I am well enough. Thank you for the tea." Olaug stood on shaky legs. "You know Ull is going to be very angry with us when he finds out what we are doing."

"If Ull's angry, it means Ull's alive. That's all we're trying to do; preserve our worlds. He'll be upset, but he'll understand." I carried Olaug's teacup to the kitchenette, and came back with a frown. "Where's Elsker? Isn't she coming?" When Ull had talked to her yesterday, she'd promised to be at Ýdalir to help.

"She was called away."

"By Odin?"

"He wants the Norns working together. In case . . ." Olaug looked down.

"I see." It didn't take a great visionary to piece that one together. In case I failed. Or was kidnapped. Or killed. Odin needed a backup plan in case I couldn't finish my job. But *I* needed a teacher: someone to guide me through a journey this enormous. How was I supposed to go to the darkest part of the tenth realm without Elsker? What if I screwed this up?

"You can instruct me just as well from that chair." I pointed. "Sit back down, Olaug. You're going to need your strength—I have a feeling we're in for a long night."

CHAPTER NINE

I HAD NO IDEA how right I'd been when I'd predicted a long night. Seven hours into our trial, it hit me that there was a very high probability I could fail.

"Again," Olaug instructed. I closed my eyes tight. This was excruciating. We'd worked through the night and made only marginal progress. Olaug was unrelenting in her guidance, pushing me to take the visions again and again. Thankfully, I hadn't physically transported anywhere, so in that way things were going well. Now that I was a goddess, I could tap into Asgard's magic, and I hadn't revealed myself to any giants or dark elves.

Yet.

But every journey to the tenth realm left me weak and more exhausted. And though I described everything as I saw it, Olaug's transcriptions left us little to go off. I wasn't sure where to find Asgard's enemies, and though the whole purpose of this alternate plane was to provide information, it sure wasn't coughing any up for me. Everything I saw was hazy, and the places I went weren't familiar at all.

It didn't take long to figure out that Ull and Olaug had kept me from the darkest creatures of their world. They were way more terrifying than the monsters I'd conjured in my dreams, and left me with no doubt that my nightmares were about to come true. I willed myself to the scariest demons, returning again and again in a failed attempt to crack their plan. By dawn, my mind was filled with visions of wicked giants, cold and steely in their determination to kill my family; bloodthirsty animals led by the oversized talking wolf who planned the brutal massacre of those I held most dear; and the deadly tree-trunk serpent who let out a guttural hiss through fangs so large, I knew he would kill anything the others missed. I saw them all, but in spite of Olaug's coaching I could not see how or when they would move to destroy us. I had no idea how to protect Asgard.

And it was nearly dawn.

Panting, I wiped my face and moved to sit on the couch in the hidden room beneath the library. "No, Kristia," Olaug said brusquely. "You have to push on. You are the secret weapon none of the Fates could see. Again."

I squeezed my eyes shut, fighting against the needles piercing my skull. It was excruciating to maintain this level of focus. When I forced the visions, they hurt. A lot. Every muscle in my body ached, and I felt like a fiery poison had been poured directly down my spine and was making its way through my extremities with agonizing slowness. But I had to keep going. The fate of our worlds rested on my exhausted shoulders.

Summoning my last bit of strength, I furrowed my brow. The needles seared through my brain, but I ignored them. I drew on everything Elsker had showed me the morning of my wedding, and everything Olaug had reiterated tonight. I focused on the quiet center in my head. Immediately I pictured the beach from our honeymoon. I stood where the warm, blue water lapped against the white sand and focused on my breathing. *In and out. In and out.* When I felt centered, I pictured the enormous redwood engulfing my body, shooting to the center of the earth and anchoring me with its roots. My body was grounded.

I placed the protection around my aura and left my body. I kept contact with the cord, like Elsker instructed. These were scary times, and who knew what darkness was waiting on the other side?

I was about to find out.

I stepped outside Ýdalir, and found myself in a fog. The haziness slowly gave way to the crystal clear night of a world far away. The cord stretched up, and I floated after it, traveling just below the clouds. I scanned the ground beneath me searching for . . . for what? How was I supposed to find what I was looking for when I didn't even know what it was? This was a glaring oversight in the Fates' plan. I didn't know who our enemies were, what they looked like, or where they would be. I was failing Asgard miserably.

As the thought made its way across my battered brain, my spirit moved through the cracked window of a worn building.

I was in a big, cold hall, and the grumbling of a small group drew me to the corner. I hesitated; did they know I was there? A stumpy man looked quickly in my direction, but he returned to the muffled conversation in front of him. He sounded like he was underwater. I stayed where I was, listening.

The muted sounds grew less murky as the seconds ticked by and for the first time I could hear their voices clearly. Finally. I focused on their words.

"By midnight tomorrow, Asgard will fall."

Hot potato, this was it—the meeting I'd been searching for. I held my breath as I waited for more.

"Which of Asgard's entrances are weakest?" A disgusting creature covered in boils spoke in a gravelly voice. Entrances? Plural? That couldn't be. The Bifrost was the only way in.

"We can use the bridge if you let me kill Heimdall," said a dwarf. His voice had all the warmth of nails on a chalkboard, and the pounding in my head began with a vengeance.

"No," a cloaked figure interrupted. "I will kill Heimdall and open the Bifrost myself. I'll break into Odin's Chamber first and cut off Frigga's head on my way in." The group grumbled in surprise; the chamber entrance was news to them, too.

"Are you sure, Loki?" the boiled creature shrieked.

The figure pulled back his hood to reveal features

that looked all too familiar to me. It was Elf Man. He was the cretin orchestrating this plot against Asgard; the fiend draining the life out of my beloved Olaug; the demon trying to destroy my husband, my family, and both of our realms. And even worse, Elf Man was Loki, an Asgardian himself. He'd made sure Balder was killed, and he'd tried to do the same to me. I moved my hand to rub my temples, the pounding intensifying as I pieced together the things Loki had said in my visions. Somehow he'd known that if Ull married me I would mess up his whole Ragnarok attack.

Oh Lord, he'd already tried to murder me. What would he do if he found me spying on him now? I forced myself to stay very still.

"Dismembered Frigga." Loki's voice was smooth. "How better to show Asgard we have control?"

The huge wolf that had killed me a dozen different ways over the years let out a bark.

"What is it, Fenrir?" Loki asked. The wolf rose from the floor where he was resting. He let out a series of growls that made my insides cringe.

"Yes, my son. You may slay Odin in his chamber," Loki praised. "A most excellent idea. I taught you well. Yes, Jörmungandr?"

The enormous snake that destroyed me whenever the wolf had failed let out a low hiss.

"No, my son, your brother is to slay Odin. You may devour Thor."

The wolf and the snake were Loki's children? Something resembling recognition clicked inside.

"Loki." A misshapen giant stood. "Let me sail the

118

ship *Naglfar*. It will open the sky and provide access to the Bifrost. Once we cross, the bridge will break under our weight. Asgard will be isolated and defenseless."

"I wondered which of you would be brave enough to steer the ship." Loki smiled cruelly. "I accept your offer. And then, my friends, we gather on the battlefield of Asgard to attack. When victory is ours, we burn the earth and swallow the sky."

I was sick. What he described was the exact vision from my nightmares.

"But what about their defense? I heard they have a new weapon; a seer who can overpower us all." The dwarf looked around with suspicion and I held my breath.

"Their defense? Oh, friends." Loki shook his head in condescension. "Their defense is an untrained, unprepared human. Her skills depend on the teaching of an old goddess who has, unfortunately, been infected with my Crushing Curse. She will be too weak to teach the human now. First her spirit will go, then her body, as her bones implode. When there is nothing left she will plead for death, and I will be only too happy to grant her final wish." He chuckled darkly. "No, friends, the old one will not be able to help their seer. She will be as inept as she always was."

Ouch.

"But what if the old one is healed?"

"Ah, the beauty of the Crushing Curse. It has only two cures: the death of the one who cast it, or possession of a magical artifact. Asgard will never defeat me, so the first is not an option. And nobody has

119

seen the missing artifact in decades. No, the old one will be dead within two dawns. Now, do any of you have any intention of losing this battle?" The monsters erupted in deafening cries as Loki threw his arms up in a victorious salute.

I had to get out of there. I turned and started to fly out of the building, but something held me back. I glanced down and squinted—something was moving just behind a locked door.

"Help!" The faint cry was familiar. Elsker.

It may well have been a trap. Olaug had spent a good portion of the evening making sure I understood how my body would suffer if my spirit got stuck on this plane—I'd lose my powers, I'd be susceptible to illness, and my immortality could be compromised. Not to mention that if someone kidnapped me here they'd have control over my abilities in every other realm. They could use my visions to do whatever they wanted to everyone I loved . . . and execute Ragnarok with the benefit of all-knowing sight. Therefore it was imperative I get out of the tenth realm unharmed.

But there was no way I was going to leave the woman responsible for my happiness trapped in this godforsaken warehouse. I floated back down and crouched outside the closet.

"Elsker? Is that you?" I kept my voice low and my eyes on the gathering in the main room.

"Kristia? Oh gods. You must get out of here." Her voice was muffled but I could hear fear.

"No way. I'm not leaving without you. We have to break you out of that room." I glanced around. A thin

silver rope with one frayed end lay just outside the door. "Holy cow. Elsker, did they sever your cord?"

"Yes. Now go. If they sever yours it will be nearly impossible for us to find our way home."

Crumbs on a cracker. My gaze landed on a rusty metal crowbar propped up in a corner. It wasn't ideal but it would do. Careful not to make too much noise, I wedged it against the hinges and pushed. The door didn't budge. I leaned into the bar with all my weight, and the door moved a fraction of an inch.

"I'm trying to break you out, but this door is stuck."

"Try the lock," Elsker mumbled.

"What do you mean?"

"Smash the lock. I saw it before they tossed me in here; it's old and it will break."

"But the noise will draw their attention," I whispered back.

"Then we'll have to fly like Helheim the minute the door opens. Do you see my cord?"

"It's right here—just outside the door." I assessed the lock, looking for the best angle of impact. I had one shot at this thing. "What happened?"

"Odin sent me on an information recon and I landed here, but they found me and cut my cord. I can follow it back to my body if I can get to it, but we have to move fast. Who knows what they will do with my spirit when they come back for me?"

Frost wove an intricate pattern between my vertebrae, coating my spine in an icy chill. I shook the feeling off. "It's not going to come to that."

"Just get us out of here. And if it comes down to it,

take off without me. You are far more valuable to them than I am. Asgard needs you."

Did she know me at all?

"Absolutely not. We're getting out of here together. Now I'm going to count to three and spring you. One." I eyed the lock and took aim. "Two. Three!"

I swung at the lock and a deafening clang rang through the warehouse. Thirty pairs of beady eyes trained on me and I ripped the lock from the door and pulled the handle. Elsker tumbled out and grabbed her cord. She wrapped it tightly around her waist in a knot that would have made my old scout troop leader proud.

"Fly!" Elsker ordered. She reached for my hand and pulled me up after her. We shot from the ground through the window as the demons thundered after us.

"Which way did they go?" a grating voice cried. In seconds they were right behind us, and closing in.

"What do we do?" I asked Elsker.

"When I give the signal, turn and hold your palm to them. I want you to picture a lion charging at them, teeth bared, ready to pounce. Push that image out from your hands. Can you do it?" She didn't stop moving as she spoke.

"Yes," I panted.

"Okay . . . now!" Elsker shouted.

We stopped and turned toward the pursuing mob, palms out to project the image. I saw not one, but nine giant cats leap from our hands and bear down on the group. There wasn't time to process the absolutely insane fact that my hands could congure magical attack animals in this realm. And there wasn't time to absorb the shrieks of fear or the crunching of bones as the lions picked off the demons one by one, flinging their remains to the dusty ground until only a dozen of the monsters remained. Every bit of energy I could muster was focused on our escape.

"Now fly!" Elsker grabbed my hand and took off again. We shot through the air.

"Follow the light," Elsker hissed and we directed our cords skyward. Up, up, until we reached a doorway nearly exploding with brightness. "Go through."

"You first." I opened the door and shoved her inside, tumbling after her.

"My path leads back to Asgard—my body is there, under Odin's protection. Get back to your body quickly. And thank you." Elsker gave me a nod and shot off to the left. I heard footsteps behind me but I didn't turn to see which of the monsters was tracking me. I raced to the right until I saw the gates of Ýdalir. I flew through, back down to the chamber, and climbed back into my body.

I'd made it. But it had come at a price.

CHAPTER TEN

THE VISION WAS TOO much. My head spun, the needles now machetes hacking my frontal lobe, and without knowing how I got there I was back with Olaug, crouching on the floor. My entire body was covered in sweat and the only thing I wanted was sleep. It had been worth it. In the same way I had known so many things, I was positive this was the vision I was meant to see—the one with the potential to alter Ragnarok, to save Asgard and Earth.

Olaug handed me a glass of water and a towel. As I gulped it down, I panted. Words gushed out of me in a downpour as I relayed the events I'd seen. "Did you get all of that?"

Olaug's grim nod confirmed my hope—this was our enemies' battle plan. It was what we had been waiting for.

Without a word, she strode to the laptop that was her lifeline to Asgard. Odin came to the screen. He looked very different than he had at our wedding. His face seemed much older now, lined with the stresses of the past few weeks. His expression was guardedly hopeful.

"*Ja?*" he asked in Norse.

"It is time," Olaug replied. "Kristia has seen the plans."

"*Bare bra*—very well. Kristia, stay at Ýdalir and wait for Ull. You shall be protected; our enemies would make terrible use of your gift. Olaug, come to me the moment Ull returns. Tyr and I will finalize our strategy when you arrive. And Kristia." Odin's voice softened. "Thank you. You have done us all a great service."

I was too exhausted to do more than nod but Odin's gratitude touched me. I knew it had taken a lot for him to welcome me to his family.

"I will await your arrival, Olaug." He signed off.

Moments later, Ull climbed out of the chamber in the wall. He looked like he'd been to hell and back. His shirt was caked in blood, and there were speckles of crimson in his hair that I seriously doubted were barbeque sauce. If the way he limped through the door was any indication, he had to be in an enormous amount of pain.

"Oh Ull!" I tried to stand to help him, but I was too weak to do more than push myself up on my elbow. When Ull's eyes fell on me, still crumpled on the ground, he rushed to my side in a panic.

"Kristia, are you all right? Is she all right?" He turned on Olaug. "What happened to her? Great Odin, why is she curled up like that?" He dropped to kneel beside me. "Darling, I am so sorry I left you here. Can you move? Are you hurt?" Turning on Olaug again, he thundered furiously, "What happened to my wife?"

I lifted a shaky finger to his lips. Even in this state, just touching their soft perfection was almost too much. I pulled his face to mine with all the strength I had left and kissed him.

"I'm all right, Ull. I promise. But are you? You look like . . . what happened to you?"

He ignored my question. Instead he breathed with relief, scooping me off the floor to cradle me in his arms. "What is going on?" It was directed at Olaug; he couldn't ask any more of me.

"Are you okay, Ull?" Olaug's face formed a mask of concern as she took in his appearance.

"I am fine. My concern is for Kristia."

Olaug nodded. "Her visions worked. She saw the meeting. She has seen what we need to win." Olaug quickly described my revelation, and Ull's eyes grew.

"Kristia, you promised you would not do anything risky. If I had known you were planning to do this tonight, I would have watched over you."

"I didn't want you to worry about me. You have so much to deal with, I couldn't give you anything else."

"Oh, Kristia." He buried his head in my hair. Any other man would have looked at my exhausted form and said 'I told you so,' but my bloody warrior just held me. "You can *always* talk to me. Please do not take on such an enormous burden on your own, ever again."

"But I wasn't on my own." I pointed out. "Olaug was with me. Elsker was too, kind of. She was trapped in the tenth realm, but we got her out. Ull, breathe! I promise, she's okay. We all are."

Ull's gratitude toward his grandmother was matched only by his irritation. "Then both of you must promise to include me in your schemes from now on. Please." His concern as he took in my sweat-soaked body was evident. "This took far too much from you, my love."

How could he say that? Ull's burdens over the past few months had far exceeded mine. His hands trembled, though with fear for my welfare or exhaustion from whatever he had been doing in Asgard, I couldn't say. It didn't matter; we couldn't afford any weakness now. The crux of our battle was only beginning. Olaug had to leave right away to get word to Odin so he, Thor, Sif, and the strongest warriors could move to destroy the creatures I'd seen.

"Wait—Olaug," I whispered. She paused on wobbly legs. "Forget what that creep said. Nothing is going to happen to you."

"What did what creep say?" Ull asked.

"I'll explain later." I squeezed his hand and turned to Olaug. "You're going to be just fine. I know what we have to do to fix this, and I promise we'll set this right."

Olaug nodded and turned to the Bifrost. With utmost care she grasped her notes in her hands, entered the chamber, and spoke the oath of fealty to Asgard that Heimdall required before opening the bridge.

When she was gone, Ull cradled me tightly, stroking my hair as he rocked back and forth.

"Explain. What is happening with Olaug?"

"Oh, Ull. It's awful. Elf Man cast the Crushing Curse on her—and unless we kill him, she's going to die!"

"No," Ull growled.

"And there's more. Turns out Elfie is Loki. He's the one who's been coming after me in my visions. And he's the one who cursed Olaug—he's the reason she's sick. I'm sorry I didn't realize who he was before."

Ull sucked in air. His eyes narrowed to slits and I was fairly positive he would have shot daggers from them if he could. "That venomous backstabbing . . . after all Odin has done for him." He shook his head. "Well, you are safe now. He will never get through me. And we will set things right for Olaug." Ull's hands cradled my body, and his blue eyes bored into mine with such intensity my mind was wiped clean. "Kristia Myhr," he murmured, in a tone that wasn't altogether reproachful. "What were you thinking? You scared me half to death."

"I'm sorry, Ull, I really am. But I couldn't give you anything more to worry about."

He eyed me with admiration. "And I thought you could not get any braver."

"Speaking of brave, why is there blood in your hair?" My voice cracked. "And all over your shirt?"

"There was a situation."

"I thought Odin was just giving you busy work so I could do my whole Seer thing?"

"Hardly," Ull snorted. "I would have seen through that. No, my dear, we were overcome by *ikkedød*."

"*Ikkedød*?"

"How do I explain?" Ull looked to the ceiling. "They are a hybrid of demons; undead warriors of Helheim's mistress, Hel."

I shuddered. "What do they do?"

"The better question is what do they not do?" Ull shrugged. "They are shape shifters; mood influencers who steal their victims' souls by sucking their energy right out of their bodies; and intensely efficient fighting machines. They can overpower their prey in the amount of time it takes most gods to draw their weapons. If an *ikkedød* wants you dead, it is nearly impossible to survive."

My breath caught. "Then how are you here?"

"I said they could overpower *most gods*. It would take a lot more than Hel's minions to keep me from my girl."

"Oh, Ull." I held my hands to his cheeks and pressed my forehead against his. I wished I could have been with him to help him through whatever nightmare he'd just endured. I probably wouldn't have been of much use, but I hated knowing he'd been on his own.

Except he hadn't been on his own. Gunnar and a team of warriors had been with him. They'd already taken down a dozen of the monsters and were making sure the forest was clear when one dropped in on Ull and stabbed him right in the—

I pulled my face away from Ull's and lowered my

hands. My voice was far shriller than I meant for it to be when I demanded, "Show me your stomach."

Ull lifted his shirt over his head and tossed it on the ground. "It is not the ideal time to be romantic, but I am always in the mood if you—"

"That's not what I mean. Good Lord, Ull." I ignored the streaks of blood that covered his chest like war paint. Instead, my fingers reached out to hover over the gaping wound on his midsection. "No wonder you're so bloody. We have to get this stitched up. I can't believe that demon stabbed you with a tree. *A tree.* Seriously?"

"It was a large branch, maybe a few inches in diameter. Not a tree." Ull stilled. "And how did you know that?"

"I . . . I saw it. When I touched your face." I jumped up and ran for the tiny kitchen. "We can talk about that later. I need to get you fixed up. Why isn't that healing?"

Ull shrugged. "It was probably laced."

"With what?" The banging of the cupboard doors echoed through the chamber as I tore the space apart. "Where in the name of all that is good and holy do you people keep your first-aid kit? It isn't anywhere in here! And why are you laughing?"

"Because." Ull crossed the room and stood beside me. His biceps flexed as he placed his hands on the kitchen counter. "I do not need a first-aid kit. The *ikkedød* probably laced their weapons with some kind of poison, which accounts for the slow healing. Toxins affect us, just as they affect humans. But Heimdall

130

injected us with a repulsion serum when we crossed the Bifrost. Any object, liquid or gaseous that enters my bloodstream in the next twenty-four hours will automatically eject itself within a quarter of a day. Most poisons take longer than that to damage our cellular structure—a perk of immortality. So while this is inconvenient, and not all together comfortable, it is not something that requires a first-aid kit."

My hands wrapped firmly around my waist and I tapped my foot. "First of all, that is seriously ingenious of Heimdall. And second, I'm your wife, and you're bleeding. Humor me. Where is the kit?"

Ull sighed, then returned to the couch. "Second shelf, cabinet to the left of the sink, in the back."

"Thank you." I found what I was looking for, then ran a clean towel under warm water. Ull raised an eyebrow as I approached, but he didn't object when I knelt in front of him. "Oh, Ull. This looks terrible."

"I have had worse." He winced as I dabbed at the wound.

"It hurts," I sympathized. "This will hurt more. Sorry." Ull rested his head on the back of the couch as I poured rubbing alcohol on a fresh towel. He sucked in a sharp breath as I pressed it against his stomach. "I'm sorry," I apologized again.

"I can take it," he muttered.

It took a few minutes to clean the wound, and by the time I'd removed most of the blood I could see the actual injury looked smaller. The flesh was slowly knitting itself back together. At this rate, it would be nothing more than a memory by the time I put away the medical kit.

"You weren't kidding. Whatever Heimdall gave you is working."

"I know." Ull held out his arms. I climbed onto the couch and snuggled against his naked chest. "What I do not know is how you saw inside my head. Your visions do not usually work like that, do they?"

"I didn't think so," I admitted. What had I been doing when I saw the *ikkedød* drop out of the tree and stab Ull? Had it been the way I touched him? Or was it the intention behind my thoughts? "Can I try again?"

Ull ran his fingers along my hairline. "Be my guest."

I sat up and cupped Ull's cheeks, placing my forehead to his, like I'd done before. I focused on remembering the image I'd seen of Ull, Gunnar and the *ikkedød*, and suddenly Ýdalir disappeared. Instead, I had a panoramic view of a moonlit forest.

It was cold; a thick fog settled around my legs, obscuring my view of everything from waist-level down. Not far away, I could see ten gods moving slowly through the darkness. They wore black, and carried weapons of varying sizes—Gunnar held his cross-bow at eye level, Ull carried a broad sword. Another held two daggers, while one had a mace. They crept on silent feet, shifting their attention with each tree they passed. They kept glancing up, though nothing in the forest moved.

"This quadrant's clear," Gunnar called.

Ull nodded. "They must have gone underground. Regroup and head for the south fork. We will sweep the riverbank, then report back to Odin in—"

Before he could finish, something dropped out of a tree. It lunged as it fell, impaling Ull's stomach with a branch.

"Faen," Ull swore. He doubled over, clutching his arms across his torso as a dozen other figures fell from the trees. They were gnarled; flesh and bandages hung off exposed bone as if they'd been decaying for decades. But any resemblance to the dead stopped there. These creatures moved fast, struck faster and looked like they were designed for destruction. They were disgusting, deadly, and absolutely terrifying.

Ull pulled the branch out of his stomach with a deep groan. "Elite Team, strike . . . now!"

The warriors jumped to action. Blades swung as metal clashed with exposed bone. Some the ikkedød dropped into the fog, cut in half by the enraged assassins. But the others swirled in a mist that blended with the fog, disappearing completely.

"Regroup," Ull commanded. The warriors formed a tight circle at his side.

"You okay, mate?" Gunnar nudged Ull with his elbow. He never lowered his crossbow as his eyes scanned the trees for another attack.

"Fit as a fiddle," Ull grunted, shifting his sword in his hand.

"Kristia's little idioms rubbing off on you?" Gunnar's game face disappeared as he broke into a smirk.

"Shove it," Ull retorted. "My two o'clock."

The warriors turned as a unit, and charged at the figures emerging from the fog. The ikkedød came in the form of bushes but when Gunnar fired a series of arrows the foliage exploded, leaving behind nothing more than the stench of decay.

"Was that all of them?" Gunnar turned a full circle, never lowering his crossbow.

"Anders is on stats. What was the projection?" Ull turned to the ginger-haired god next to him.

"An attack unit should have held a dozen."

"And how many went down?"

"By my count? Eleven."

"Dritt," Ull swore.

Gunnar stalked toward the nearest boulder. He leaped into the air and came down, crushing it with his bow. The rock dissipated, and shards of granite flew in all directions.

"Was that it?" one of the warriors called.

"Naw. No stench." Gunnar threw his fist at a tree. The impact left a deep hole, but the tree remained standing. "Come out, come out, wherever you are," he warbled.

"That should send it running. Is that your plan? Flush it out with bad singing?" Ull swung his sword at a shrub, chopping off seven inches.

"Maybe." Gunnar grinned. "You got a better plan?"

"Get down!" Ull yelled. Gunnar dropped to the ground without question, disappearing beneath the fog as a rotting figure flew out of the trees. It dove after Gunnar, and for a moment all I could see was the ripple of the mist as god and monster struggled underneath. Ull charged across the forest. He leapt at the spot I'd last seen Gunnar, arms and legs outstretched. There was a heavy thud as he struck the ground, followed by the raking sound of metal on bone. For a brief moment I could see Ull's sword poke through the vapor before it disappeared again. Then I heard the sound of metal piercing flesh, followed by a thick gurgling; it sounded like a clogged sink. In a flash I surmised someone was choking on his or her own blood, and my stomach clenched as I waited to see whom it was. I hadn't seen Gunnar in more than a minute.

Ull's sword flew out of the fog, the final ikkedød still attached to the blade. It struck the thick trunk of the nearest tree, pegging the monster to the trunk. Before I could blink, the demon vaporized, leaving nothing more than a heinous odor behind.

My eyes combed through the haze, searching for the spot Ull and Gunnar had been. I waited for what felt like an interminable period, but the mist stayed as still as the Nehalem River at low tide. Ull's team closed in, canvassing the ground through three feet of pea-soup fog. As they searched, a movement caught my eyes. A tousled, blond head rose from the mist, followed by thick shoulders, and finally a strong torso. Ull stood, carrying Gunnar in his arms. Our friend's chest was covered in blood, and his eyes were tightly closed. His left arm hung limp at his side, sliced so deep I got an anatomy lesson much more vivid than anything I'd had in school. Before it had been destroyed, the ikkedød had sliced clean through Gunnar's tendons.

"Is the forest clear?" Ull barked. Without waiting for an answer, he lowered his head and started to run.

His team followed suit. "Yes, sir."

"Then move out. Gunnar needs a healer."

"He took the serum." Anders jogged along side Ull. "It should expel the venom."

"It should," Ull agreed. "But that does him no good if he bleeds out first. Gunnar saved my life on more than one occasion. He is not going to die tonight. Someone retrieve my sword. I need to move."

With that Ull flew through the forest. By the time he broke through the fog, his feet moved so fast I couldn't see their movement. He disappeared from my view.

"Tell me he's okay." My eyes flew open as I pulled my face away from Ull's. "If anything ever happened to Gunnar . . ."

"He is fine." Ull nodded. "Idunn extracted the venom, performed a transfusion, and stitched his wounds. She reattached the tendon first, so he will have full use of his arm within half a day. Did you know she was a neurosurgeon?"

"I think someone mentioned it once." The backs of my arms tingled. Ull still didn't know the full extent of what Idunn had to do to my brain to make me immortal. And I intended to keep it that way.

"Gunnar will appreciate your concern."

"Jeez, Ull. Those things are terrifying. Did you kill all of them?"

Ull grimaced. "All Hel sent, yes. But do you believe the ruler of the underworld only has two units of demons in her charge?"

"No," I whispered. "What are we going to do?"

"The only thing we can do." Ull shrugged. "We will take this one battle at a time. You performed brilliantly tonight, Kristia. You secured the intel we needed to disable the opposition. Now Odin will confer with our war god, Tyr, and we will follow orders. There is nothing more we can do tonight."

Ull wrapped an arm around my shoulder and pulled me to him. I rested my cheek on his bare shoulder, relishing the familiar smell of pine and soap. My eyelids grew heavy as the stress of the night overtook me. Before I nodded off, I felt Ull's lips brush my forehead.

"Kristia, what you did tonight was incredibly brave . . . but doing it without me here to protect you. . . well, do not *ever* worry me like that again," he commanded fiercely. "I could not live without you."

"Don't ever worry *me* like that again!" I countered. "Mythological zombie demons, and Gunnar nearly losing his arm, and you showing up looking like death warmed over . . . just promise me you'll be careful. I need you."

"Deal." Ull squeezed me tight.

I buried my head in his chest, giving in to my exhaustion. I closed my eyes, and within moments fell into a deep sleep.

❄ ❄ ❄ ❄

Ull's mobile woke me too soon, and he eyed it with annoyance.

I smiled groggily. "Perfect timing."

"Hardly. You were sleeping."

I pulled my wrap sweater around me before running my hand across Ull's abdomen. The skin was clean and firm; there was no evidence of the gruesome wound he'd just incurred. "Do you want me to run upstairs and get you a shirt? I don't want you to catch cold."

"I am fine, sweetheart." Ull kissed the top of my head. "Besides, Olaug is here."

Ull shifted me in his arms as the portal opened and Olaug stepped out. She didn't waste a minute. She hurried across the room and began tacking pins to the map on the wall, demonstrating our counterattack. Ull and I exchanged a sideways glance. Under Tyr's direction, Odin, Thor, and Sif were hard at work to thwart the jotuns' onslaught. It would be easy enough now that they knew which elements would move together to break the Bifrost, and which monsters would mount attacks on the key Asgardians. Tyr had orchestrated a plan for him and Odin to sink the ship before it could break its moorings, preventing the invasion of the Bifrost and blocking the primary entrance to Asgard. Heimdall would keep guard at the bridge to make sure unwanted visitors were denied access, and two members of the Elite Team were assigned to protect the Bifrost's protector. The secret entrance to Odin's chamber was sealed. A team of warriors would wait there for Loki. Thor would lead the attack on the serpent and the wolf. Once they were dead Odin would sever Jotunheim from Earth and Asgard, cutting off access between the realms. Ull would stay at Ýdalir to protect me from Loki. We all knew the idea of my visions would be too tempting for him to ignore. And the remainder of Asgard's considerable guard had been dispatched to suppress skirmishes breaking out near key inter-realm portals.

There were three teams of warriors stationed in Muspelheim, where Surtr had assembled a batallion of fire giants and was preparing to launch an all out attack on Asgard. Two more teams of warriors were stationed in Jotunheim, and another pair was en route to Helheim. Peacekeeping squadrons were traveling to allied realms, and the Elite Team was manning the Dark Forest. Every precaution had been taken. If things went according to plan, Ragnarok would be won without the loss of one Asgardian or human life. It was almost too good to be true.

Our waiting game began.

CHAPTER ELEVEN

I WOKE UP EARLY on Thursday morning, filled with more nerves than I'd had at my first middle school dance; it was going to be a very long day. My new family would be fighting for their lives and I couldn't do anything but wait. Neither Ull nor I were supposed to leave the cottage in case Loki was watching. I'd done as much as I could to help Asgard, and now our future was in the hands of the more experienced fighters. I knew they'd be able to rise to the occasion, but it was still unnerving to have to wait for news.

I focused on Ull. Even in sleep his powerful muscles seemed tensed for battle, his strong jaw firmly clenched, and his bare chest rising rhythmically. My breath caught in my throat, and I reached out to touch him. He wrapped an arm around me, murmuring my name as he woke. I snuggled into his chest and wrapped my fingers around his bicep, holding on tight. For the next half-hour we lay quietly in the pre-dawn light, listening to the birds, hoping fervently that this was not the last morning we would spend together.

❋ ❋ ❋ ❋

When Ull's mobile rang later that morning, I jumped so high I nearly spilled my tea.

"*Ja*," he answered cautiously. He pushed his own mug across the dining room table and glanced out the window toward the garden. When he pressed a finger to the phone, Olaug's voice came through the speaker, loud enough for me to hear.

"Tyr and Odin are preparing to attack the ship so it cannot sail for the Bifrost. They will depart from Asgard this afternoon. Thor and Sif are on their way to the battlefield to meet the serpent and the wolf, but they do not anticipate any problems killing their charges."

"And Loki?" Ull was guarded.

"Nobody has heard from him." Olaug sounded worried. "Naturally, he is no longer permitted in Asgard. We do not know whether he is aware of our attacks. I will return to Ýdalir immediately to wait for news with you. Odin will send reinforcements to guard Kristia as soon as he can spare them."

"I appreciate that. Travel safely." As Ull hung up the phone, I wondered who Loki would go after first— now it was a question of when, not if, he would come for us.

"It's scary," I whispered.

Ull reached over and rubbed my shoulder softly. "You do not have anything to worry about, darling.

Loki cannot get to you, or to me, for that matter, so long as we stay within Ýdalir's borders. I set protective enchantments around the property so no unwanted visitors can enter. We are perfectly safe here. But do not, under any circumstances, cross the borders. Is that clear?"

I nodded. I felt oddly secure, considering the enormity of what was most likely coming for us.

"Strange." Ull stared at his phone.

"What is it?"

"I have not heard from Gunnar since last night. Once Idunn cleared him, he was supposed to collect Inga and bring her here until the Loki situation was sorted." His finger tapped the screen.

I chewed my thumbnail. "When should they have gotten here?"

Ull continued his tapping. "When I left Asgard he was healing. Idunn said it would only be another half hour before he could be released. Inga was out on assignment, but she was due back shortly. They should have been in Bibury this morning."

Our eyes met, the air between us thick with anxiety. Dagnabbit, this was so not good.

"You have to make sure they're okay, Ull. Take the Bifrost. Go."

"Absolutely not. I am not leaving you alone. Never again."

"Well then, I'll go check on them."

"Kristia, no. It is not safe. We will think of another way to make sure they are all right." Ull squeezed my arm.

142

"There's no other way, Ull. Everyone else is fighting, or traveling to their fight, or whatever. Listen, you're right—I don't really want to be all by myself here; not if there's a chance Loki could come back. So I'll go look for Gunnar and Inga. You're here to guard my body. And I've got this tenth realm thing down pat. I'll be fine."

"Yes, but—"

"But nothing. If our friends need us, we can't exactly sit around here drinking tea." I gestured to my cup. "I can check on them and get back to you in less than five minutes. And if anything is wrong, we'll know we need to figure out some way to send help. Maybe there's a junior Valkyrie on a coffee break somewhere, or something."

Ull let out a long-suffering sigh. "You are going to send me to an early grave, worrying about you. You do realize this?"

"I learned from the best." I shrugged. "I'm going now."

"Please be careful," Ull urged. "If anything were to happen to you . . ."

"Nothing's going to happen. You're stuck with me, remember?" I pressed his fingers to my lips.

"Still. At least let me hold you while you do this. And come back immediately when you locate them. I want to know where to be able to find you if something goes wrong."

My eyebrows shot up. "Anything else, Captain?"

"Yes. Do not get hurt."

"Aye-aye." I gave a mock salute as I rose from my

chair and climbed onto Ull's lap. He wrapped thick arms around me and rested his cheek on the top of my head. "I'll be back in a jiffy."

"You had better be," Ull growled.

"Stuck with me," I reminded him as I ducked my head against his chest. Then I took a long breath, grounded myself, and let my spirit take flight.

My search didn't take long. I went straight to Asgard's healing unit. Gunnar wasn't there, but it looked like I'd just missed him. The bed under the window still had medical equipment nearby, and there was an indentation in the pillow.

"Where did he go?" Anders stood at the foot of the bed, blinking.

"I have no idea." Idunn strolled into the room, looking equally surprised. "His wound was nearly resealed—I told him he needed one final dose before I could discharge him, and he yelled for me to hurry. Something about Inga being in trouble." She held up the loaded syringe in her hand. "Looks like he couldn't wait."

Anders backed out of the room. "Where is Inga?"

Idunn moved to the next bed and positioned a domed screen over another injured god. "I don't know. But if you see Gunnar, let him know he needs to come back for this." She set the syringe on the table by the empty bed. "If he doesn't complete the course, he'll be susceptible to infection."

"Will do." Anders turned on one heel and bolted from the room. With one last look at the row of injured Asgardians lining the healing unit, I followed suit.

Anders took off at a full sprint toward a grove of trees. My attention shifted toward the shiny palatial structure to the north. I'd never been to Asgard in my physical form, and I was beyond curious about Ull's home realm. But in all likelihood, our friends were in trouble, and this was hardly the appropriate time for a sightseeing excursion. My eyes focused on Anders and I took to task. There would be plenty of time to explore Asgard later . . . I hoped.

Anders crossed an expansive clearing in record time, then lowered his head and charged into the trees. I dove after him, flying along behind, desperately trying to ignore the feeling in my gut. In addition to being dark, cold, and densely packed, this forest emitted a repulsive vibe, as if it were trying to eject any source of warmth or light.

It was trying to kick me out.

I pushed against the invisible, or perhaps imagined, force field. It pushed back, a none-too-gentle pressure on the top of my head as I flew after Anders. Ignoring the sensation, I moved forward until Anders skidded to a stop. I pulled up just in time, narrowly avoiding flying straight into his back. My gaze darted down when I heard Anders' shout.

"Dritt!"

Dritt indeed. I squeezed my eyes shut as I pulled myself out of the forest, traveling at light speed back to Bibury. Ull was not going to be happy.

❄ ❄ ❄ ❄

"Thank Odin." Ull kissed the top of my head as I squirmed in his arms. "You are safe."

"I'm not here long. I just wanted you to know they're in some cold, creepy forest in Asgard. It looks like the one you were in before, but it keeps trying to push me out of it. What is wrong with that place?" I turned my face up to his.

"The Dark Forest." Ull stroked my cheek with one finger. "You must be near its center. The repulsion is stronger there. What is happening in there?"

"Gunnar and Inga are fighting a monster. It's a female, about Inga's size, with dirty hair and ripped clothes. She's making these awful screeching noises and throwing flames from her hands. And she's surrounded, by those awful things that attacked you and Gunnar—the *ikkedød*. They're defending her. And there's another creature, a huge female with boils all over her skin and really unfortunate yellow teeth. She's at least twenty-feet tall."

Ull's entire body stiffened.

"What's going on?" I whispered.

"Hel."

"Ull!" He wasn't one to swear . . . in English, anyway.

"The smaller woman is Hel. Guardian of the underworld. The *ikkedød* are her minions; they're tasked with defending her. And the larger female, in all likelihood, is her mother."

"Hel has a mother?" There was no keeping the incredulity out of my voice.

"Angrboða. She is a mountain giant of questionable origin. Her union with Loki and the prophecy for their monster offspring cemented her position on Asgard's top kill-list. We have been hunting her for years."

"Wait. The giant's with Loki?"

"Yes. Hel has a father too." Ull watched me carefully as the words sank in. One more piece of the puzzle clicked into place. Fuzzy images rushed into my head. A fortress. A nursery. A wretched future for the three tiny bundles.

"Oh, shoot. Shoot, shoot." Fenrir, Jörmungandr and Hel were the children of Loki and the giant. They were the babies from my lost dreams. And they were fated to do something terrible. Only I still couldn't remember what it would be.

"Sometimes your choice of language is really quite adorable."

I ignored him. "If you've been hunting her for years, why haven't you caught her? From what I've seen, you guys are pretty thorough."

"Angrboða never leaves her palace. After she had the children, she locked the gates, hired an extensive security detail, and placed every possible protection around the property, magical and otherwise. Nobody can get within a hundred yards of her residence without being obliterated either physically, or mentally. The last time we sent a tactical team to retrieve her, half were blown to pieces and the other half came back speaking Svartish, convinced they were the house servants of a dark elf. A while back, Loki turned the children over to Odin in exchange for a cease-fire on Angrboða. We have left her alone since then."

Ull's words confirmed my suspicion. "Did you say Angrboða's palace has every possible protection?"

"Yes." Ull furrowed his brow. "Why?"

"Including a blocker?"

Recognition dawned. "Your missing visions. You were seeing Angrboða. More likely, you saw her children. She would have taken great care to cloak them from Asgardian eyes. Now your lost dreams make sense."

"You said something about a prophecy. What's that?"

Ull stroked my arm. "You are cold. Do you need a blanket?"

"What's the prophecy?" I urged. "Hurry. I need to get back to Gunnar and Inga."

"The Fates prophesied that the offspring of Loki and Angrboða would end Asgard. It was why Angrboða took such care to shield them from the gods. And it was why I have always been suspicious of Loki."

With the last piece in place, everything made sense. The three children—**Loki's children**—were destined to destroy us. I had known it all along, but I hadn't been able to understand. I was a terrible Seer. "Shoot," I whispered again. "That's what I couldn't retain in those visions. How did I let this get past me?"

Ull shook his head. "Do not dare blame yourself, my love. Blockers are powerful magic. I doubt anyone would be able to see past one."

I shook my head. "Yeah, but . . . wait, you suspected Loki all along?"

"Of course. If you knew there was a death sentence

on your children's heads, would you turn them over to the very individual who issued it?"

"Never!" I exclaimed.

"Exactly. When he heard the prophecy, Odin ordered the children killed. Angrboða locked down her palace, and nobody was able to get to them. One day out of the blue, Loki just dropped the children off at Odin's residence. The only things he asked in exchange were that Odin let the children live, and that he call off the hunt on Angrboða. That reeks of suspicion, *ja*?"

"Why didn't Odin see through that?"

"Odin can be unfortunately shortsighted. Loki has behaved erratically before, and he took this as another isolated instance. Besides, Odin had control of the demons, or so he believed, and he was confident this could mark the end of the Ragnarok prophecy. Others merely saw it as a stopping block. And many of us have been keeping a close eye on Loki, the offspring, and the giant, ever since."

"What happened to the kids?"

"Hel was cast to Helheim, and given dominion over its occupants. Protections were set so she could not leave the realm, but it would appear she has broken free. Jörmungandr was sent to the ocean of Midgard, where he grew so large he bit onto his tail. A rather fortunate curse of lockjaw has kept him there until now. And Fenrir . . . he was given a second chance. But he never changed his spots."

The wolf, the snake, and the demon. Loki's kids had haunted my dreams for years. They had killed me a hundred times while I slept. And now they were trying to destroy everyone and everything we loved.

"I have to get out of here. I have to know Gunnar and Inga are okay."

"I have to know that too. They have been my best friends all my existence. And there is nothing I would not do for them. But there has to be another way. I am sorry, Kristia. I cannot let you go back there. Hel and her mother are force enough, but combined with the *ikkedød*..."

"I know. But they're all alone. They only have Anders with them."

"Then we shall call for reinforcements. It is too dangerous for us to be apart right now." Ull eyed the closed laptop that sat on the dining room table along with our abandoned mugs of tea. "Except..."

"Except everyone's fighting. There aren't any reinforcements to call." I shook my head. "Listen, we have two choices. Either you take the Bifrost and go help them yourself—"

"I am not leaving you alone," Ull growled.

I continued as if he hadn't interrupted. "Or you let me go back there and see if they've gotten things under control. If things don't look good in the next three minutes, grab my body and come after me. And then we can help them *together*."

"Are you trying to destroy me?" Ull tipped his head back.

"I'm trying to save us. Please, let me go. Three minutes. I'll set a timer." I started to pull my phone out of my pocket.

"Flip phones do not come with timers, Kristia. We really need to update your device."

"Come on, Ull. Please. Meet me in the Dark Forest in three minutes if I'm not back. But I swear I won't take that long. If they're in trouble, I'll know it right away."

Ull's sigh let me know he'd seen reason. "Fine. But be quick. I cannot have you out of my sight any more today."

"Used my quota, huh?" I gripped his bicep and squeezed my eyes shut.

"Something like that," he muttered. But I was already gone, grounding my body and releasing my spirit.

CHAPTER TWELVE

THE FOREST HAD DROPPED *another few degrees in temperature by the time I returned. A light mist swirled across the ground, and the firm pressure worked to force me out of the space. I fought against it, staring at the scene below. If I only had three minutes, I needed to take in as much as I could.*

Four figures shifted position in the mist. Angrboða stood at the base of a tree, her head whipping from Gunnar to Inga to Anders. The three gods had formed a triangle with Gunnar running point, and they were slowly advancing on the giantess. Inga's swords were drawn, her rapier held at eye level and her dagger clutched firmly at her waist. Anders tossed a mace lightly between his hands. And Gunnar's crossbow was lined up to shoot. Hel was nowhere in sight—they must have already taken her out, although I didn't see her body anywhere. Regardless, with three-on-one odds, the giantess didn't stand a snowball's chance.

Except that she did.

Before Gunnar could fire off a shot, a half-dozen **ikkedød** *rose from the mist. They surrounded* Angrboða *in a protective circle, blocking the gods' path to their intended target. My heart lurched as the forest was filled with an overwhelming sense of desolation; the* **ikkedød were exercising their mood-altering power.**

Gunnar swore. "No matter. Close off your minds and ignore whatever they're trying to make you feel. We're doing this. On my mark."

He fired off two quick shots. The arrows pierced the undead, their corpses exploding into a gaseous mist that absolutely reeked of decay. He fired again, and two more shots eliminated two more creatures. Angrboða let out a roar, her pointed, yellow teeth flashing against her dark-purple lips. She wrapped her arms around a tree and uprooted it, then threw it at her assailants. Inga dove out of the way, but Gunnar ducked half a second too late. The tree nicked his shoulder, knocking him off balance. He went down hard, and when he pushed himself up there were sparks in his eyes.

"Now!" Gunnar shouted. He charged for the opening in the demons' defenses. The remaining two **ikkedød** *moved in front of Hel's mother, taking the form of massive boulders. Inga ran around Gunnar and delivered a fierce front-kick to one of the rocks. A small fissure formed in its center.*

"Arugh!" Inga let out a cry and kicked again, a forceful hitch that deepened the crack. "That's for hurting my husband." A front-kick. "That's for messing

with my friends." Another front-kick. "And that's for making me use my best dagger on a rock, for Helheim's sake!" With that she delivered a swift strike to the center of the break, driving her dagger deep into the stone. The boulder dissipated at the contact. "Great Odin, that stench is wretched."

"Sorry, doll," Gunnar called over his shoulder. He and Anders pummeled the remaining boulder with bare fists while *Angrboða lumbered toward another tree. "I promise we'll get you a nice, long bath when this is over. With that smelly stuff you like to put in it." Gunnar delivered another blow and the boulder crumbled, its dust blowing straight at Inga's face. Angrboða froze, the tree still rooted in the ground. She whipped her head back and forth as she took in her destroyed protectors. Her guards may have been down, but I knew better than to count her out. She crouched down and let out a growl.*

"Seriously? A bath? You'd better promise a heck of a lot more than that," Inga grumbled.

"A back rub, then? Anything you want, babe." *Gunnar let out a snarl as he moved for the giantess. He pulled his crossbow off his back and aimed for her leg. Angrboða dropped to one knee as the arrow pierced her flesh. A spray of blood shot from her thigh as she let out a shriek and lunged for Inga. Inga turned to run, but she wasn't fast enough. Enormous hands clasped around her tiny waist, and Angrboða pulled my friend off the ground.*

"Put me down, you filthy troll!" *Inga jammed her dagger into the giant's hand. It pierced the flesh* between Angrboða's thumb and forefinger, sending a stream of blood shooting straight for Inga's hair. "You have got to be kidding me."

Angrboða let out a howl. She shook her hand back and forth, probably hoping to ease the pain. The motion sent Inga flying. She landed in a crumpled heap at the base of a tree. My stomach clenched, sending a wave of nausea up my throat. A blow like that should have broken her spine.

Good thing Inga was made of tough stock.

"Anders, end the monster. Mace to the other kneecap." Gunnar shouted his order at the same time as he sprinted for Inga. He scooped her into his arms, gingerly touching the cut at her forehead. "Can you see me?"

Inga winced as she opened her eyes. "Yeah, I see you. All four of you."

"Excellent. How many fingers?" Gunnar held up his hand.

"Just one. I'm okay, Andersson. Just covered in giant blood. I think I want that bath after all." Inga let out a chuckle, then grabbed her ribs. "Ouch."

"You're not okay. You stay here while I finish this off."

"Not a chance. She made me use my dagger on a bloody rock. Chick is mine."

Gunnar shook his head but he held out his arm. "After you, my lady."

Inga pulled herself up, then adjusted her weapons. "On your count?"

Something glinted in Gunnar's eye. "One . . . two."

"Three!" Inga shouted. They turned together. As Anders delivered another blow with his mace, Gunnar fired an arrow at Angrboða's temple and Inga flew through the air, driving her rapier into the giantess' stomach. It pierced all the way to the hilt before Inga withdrew the blade and darted back. Angrboða's eyes rolled in her head. She swayed from side to side, then fell face-first into the dirt. Gunnar fired one last shot and the monster let out a low groan. Her leg twitched, and then she was still.

"Well, that was fun. Too bad the daughter got away." Gunnar slapped Inga on the behind. She turned to him with a huge smile and jumped into his arms, wrapping her legs around his waist.

Anders exhaled, his hands on his knees. "Where did Hel go?"

Inga shook her head. "No clue. We'll track her eventually. Nobody scratches my rapier and gets away with it."

"Gods, I love your vindictive streak." Gunnar grabbed Inga's ponytail and pulled her face to his. She wrapped her arms around his neck and kissed him hard on the mouth. He stumbled back a step, catching himself on the trunk of a tree. He palmed Inga's behind and whirled one-hundred-and-eighty degrees, so her back was against the bark. I averted my gaze when I heard her low moan. My three minutes were up. And from the looks of things, our friends would be just fine on their own.

"Guys." Anders' voice broke the awkward moment. "We have to get out of here. Odin needs to know what *happened."*

"We just need one more minute." Gunnar waved his hand.

"Speak for yourself," Inga mumbled.

With a smile I let the Dark Forest push me up. I soared back to my body, biting back a laugh the entire way.

"Thank Odin you are back." Ull let out a heavy sigh as I re-entered my body. "I was about to come for you."

I shifted in his arms as his face came into focus. His jaw was set and the *V* between his brows was back. My fingers traced it lightly until it disappeared. Ull might have been divine, but there was no need to encourage wrinkling.

"What happened? Are they all right?"

"They're great." I giggled. "But they're a little distracted at the moment. I wouldn't expect to hear from them any time soon."

"Should we send for reinforcements? I can get Thor on the line and—"

"Ull." I paused. There really wasn't a tactful way to put it. "They killed the giant so they're, uh, celebrating. Alone."

"Oh." Ull's eyes widened as surprise settled on his face. Then he scowled. "They pick the least appropriate times to do that. Why are you laughing?"

"Because. You're cute." I scooted up to kiss his cheek, then settled comfortably back into his lap. "The giantess is dead. The minions are too, though one scratched Inga's blade and she's seriously ticked. Hel seems to have gotten away, though. Is that bad?"

"It is not ideal." Ull stared out the window, watching the sheep in the meadow behind Ýdalir. "But it is not necessarily an imminent problem. With the *ikkedød* depleted and Angrboða out of the picture, Hel's defenses are not at their strongest. She will most likely have to sit the rest of the confrontation out while she regroups. She has never been one to fight her own battles when she has servants to do it for her."

"That's good, at least."

"What is good is that you are safely back with me. I do not like when you are gone—even when you leave a part of yourself in my arms." Ull rubbed one palm along the side of my jeans. The chill of the forest evaporated as warmth spread throughout my lower extremities.

"Can we take a break?" My voice sounded embarrassingly hopeful.

"Of course. You must be hungry. I can make us lunch." Ull stood without putting me down, moving toward the kitchen.

"Or we could do something else?" I hinted.

Ull gave me a look that bordered on shock and pride. "You are as bad as Inga. I will feed you lunch. There will be plenty of time for 'something else' after we deal with Loki."

Loki. Right. For the tiniest moment, I'd actually forgotten. "Tonight then," I acquiesced.

"Odin willing." Ull set me on the barstool at the kitchen island, then opened the refrigerator. "I have a feeling we are in for a longer day than we had imagined."

By late afternoon, we still hadn't heard anything from Sif and Thor, which worried us more than we were willing to admit. They should have killed the animals by now. Olaug was keeping herself busy in the kitchen, and Ull and I had moved outside to the garden. Ull sat on the chair by to the window, and I sat nearest the foxgloves.

We were trying to play a game of gin rummy, something I'd learned so long ago I'd forgotten completely, when we heard it. The unmistakable "pop" of a visitor's entry to Earth. Entry through the Bifrost was silent, but coming by any other means produced a distinct sound.

"Olaug," Ull called softly. "Send a message to Odin. Tell him Loki is here. Send the reinforcements." I heard her scuttle downstairs as Ull took my hand. "Do you remember what I told you?"

I nodded. We would fight as a team. I was no warrior like Sif—I would probably never be to Ull what she was to Thor. But I would stand next to my husband and defend our existence with everything I had. It was all I could do. I clasped his hand as we rose to meet our fate.

"Olaug, wait!" I cried. Her footsteps stilled; she was listening. My vision blurred violently, and I grabbed my head as I bent over.

Tyr waved an arm forward, then crept across the dock toward the boat. Odin followed his command without question, following the war god directly into a trap. Neither of them noticed the nine creatures—three jotuns, three dwarves, two trolls and a sea monster— emerging from black waters to defend the vessel.

My sight returned and I leaned on Ull, gasping with effort. "They know about the boat. They've sent guards to defend it. Make sure Odin brings warriors of his own."

Olaug nodded before she scurried off, and I could only hope that Odin would get this message before he left Asgard. The future of our worlds depended on it.

Ull helped me stand, gently massaging my aching temples and staring at me with awe. I was getting better at controlling my abilities. Ull kissed the top of my head and my mind briefly sifted through the happy memories we had shared in our home. Would we be here again when darkness fell? Or would we be somewhere very different?

The footsteps of our unwelcome visitor brought me back from my thoughts. With his arms extended as if in welcome, Loki walked toward the gate of our blossoming garden. The flowers swayed as if trying to shirk away from him. The sky dimmed from a clear blue to a murky grey. And my heart froze as I stared at the monster whose very existence made my world a living nightmare.

CHAPTER THIRTEEN

"ULL, OLD FRIEND," LOKI growled. He didn't look quite the way he had in my dreams. He was more refined today; his dark hair was slicked back, and his brown eyes pierced from beneath well-groomed brows. His ears weren't pointy anymore, either. That must have been a ruse for my benefit, to throw false light on the elves, in case I was smart enough to catch on. I wasn't. He was impeccably dressed and would have been downright attractive if I didn't know the evil inside him.

"So sorry to have missed the wedding. My invitation must have gotten lost. I was unaware you married the *human*." The word came out as a hiss, and I stepped back. Loki was quick to collect himself.

"Hello, poppet," he keened in the voice I remembered all too well. "Have you missed me?" He reached in my direction and I pulled back. The cloud over his coffee-colored eyes betrayed a dark soul.

"Long time no see, Loki." I held his gaze. Loki was unfazed.

Ull stood protectively in front of me on the cobblestone courtyard. I was next to the table under the window, holding onto the back of Ull's shirt. Fifty feet separated us from the low stone fence, and Loki stood just on the other side. Ull's fury was well contained, though the flex of his muscles reminded me that at any moment he would be prepared to strike. He planned to play this as coolly as Loki did until violence became absolutely necessary.

"Well, aren't you going to invite me in?" Loki taunted.

I knew this was the trick. He couldn't cross the threshold of the low stone fence—Ull's enchantments protected us from unwanted visitors. But if we asked him inside the garden all bets were off, and I'd be reliving the nightmare where he strangled me.

Somehow, Loki knew he needed an invite. His eyes brewed with rage when Ull sat down and pulled me onto his lap. This was part of our plan, too. Stalling would keep Loki around long enough for our reinforcements to arrive. The warriors would be here soon, and thanks to the Bifrost's silent entry we would have the element of surprise. As terrifying as this was, I was glad Loki had come. It was our best chance to capture him.

"It is far too nice a day to be indoors," Ull drawled. He twirled his finger in the air, conjuring a table and chair on the opposite side of the garden wall—just outside Ýdalir and right in front of Loki.

"Have a seat, enjoy a refreshment." Another twirl and a glass appeared on the table. Gravity of the situation aside, I was impressed. Manners and magic could commingle quite nicely.

"What brings you to Ýdalir, Loki?" Ull kept his voice calm. "One of Olaug's famous apple pies, perhaps?"

"Enough of the pleasantries, Ull." Loki stormed toward the gate, knocking the chair to the ground but stopping short when Ýdalir refused to let him in. "You know why I'm here. Your wife will be radiant spending eternity as a jotun bride. I told you I'd take you if it came to it, didn't I, poppet?"

"Didn't I already kill you twice?" I stared into his muddy eyes and held Ull's arm back as he tensed to fight. "Ull, no. Don't give him the opportunity."

Ull relaxed, eyes still on guard, and we heard angry footsteps from inside the house. Our warriors had arrived. Loki raised an eyebrow.

"Afraid to handle me on your own, Ull?" Loki's mouth curved into a sinister smirk and he snapped his fingers. A girl appeared behind him, bound, gagged, and writhing in fear. "What about you, Kristia? Would you let your friend die for you?"

He motioned with his hand and the girl screamed in agony as the ropes pulled her violently from side to side, threatening to snap her slight frame. With a shock I looked into the eyes that had held a thousand of my confidences.

"Ardis!" I screamed, running unthinkingly beyond the boundary. It was stupid, and the moment I jumped

163

over the stone fence I felt the protections of Ýdalir slipping behind me.

"Kristia!" Ull panicked. He was half a step behind me, leaping over the stone fence to tackle me to the ground. While he was still in the air, Loki snatched my wrist. I fought against him with all my strength, but I was as powerless as a tadpole in a tidal wave when he pulled me away. Ull hit the earth, grasping at the spot where I'd been.

"Kristia!" Ull let out an agonized cry and jumped to his feet. He charged after Loki, quickly closing the gap between us. I reached out for him but Loki was too fast, spinning out of his grasp and running for the trees at the edge of Bibury. His bony fingers bound my wrist tightly, cutting off the circulation in my hand. He dragged my body roughly behind him as he ran, and I screamed as I bounced off trees and rocks.

"Let go of me!" I hollered from the ground, the words coming out in gasps as my body pounded the damp earth. "Get your hands off me, you jerk! I killed you before; you know I can do it again!"

I tried to grab for my necklace, but Loki flung my body from side to side so quickly that I lost my bearings. The only sound I could hear was Loki's maniacal laughter as he taunted Ull, who fell further behind.

"I have your bride now, Ull! Once we reach the border I can transport her to Jotunheim. Isn't Odin severing it from the realms as we speak? You'll never get her back. Just think how lovely she'll look married to a jotun." He spun me onto his front, and though I clawed at his throat and screeched into his ear I could not get away. He ran easily toward the border of Bibury.

I craned my neck and saw Ull behind us. A team of Asgard's fiercest warriors sprinted after him, with Gunnar in the lead. My friend caught up to Ull, but they couldn't close the space between us. I reached for my husband, and Loki bit my left wrist with such force I couldn't lift it again. He wrapped long fingers around my right hand and wrenched me onto his back. I wanted to scream in frustration. It wasn't possible that Ull and I had made our way through so much only to be separated by a crazed lunatic. My eyes started to gloss over and the world turned the faintest shade of red.

I might have been stuck to the back of a monster, heading to the depths of hell, but I wasn't going down without a fight.

Ull had taught me to assess my situation. I was still wrapped like an unwilling koala around Loki's back, so mobility was limited. My left hand was bleeding—that weapon was out. But my right hand was strong as ever, albeit in the grasp of a sick half-jotun hell bent on killing us all. I flexed it as gently as I could. Loki was running so hard he didn't notice. I opened my palm and dug my fingernails into Loki's chest. My nails weren't long, but they'd always been strong, and I clawed at his flesh with a force that would have made a mortal cry. God skin must have been thicker, because Loki just swatted at my hand like I was an annoying fly. *Great.*

He kept my legs bound at his waist with his other hand, and I kicked at his groin as hard as I could. He skillfully tilted his pelvis, but I kept kicking and eventually landed a vital blow. Loki stumbled, nearly dropping me as he doubled over in pain. I clawed at his chest harder, trying to rake my nails up to his eyes. He held my wrist tight—he was too strong for me, so I kicked again, hoping to land a second shot. If I could just slow him up enough for Ull to catch up, I might be able to save myself.

Loki glanced back and saw Ull closing the space between us. Loki swore at me, picked himself up and took off running again. His freakishly long fingers wrapped around my feet, binding my legs around his waist and rendering me immobile. But my head was free, and I opened my mouth and bit Loki's ear so forcefully I had to spit out the chunk I took off. *Ew*. It didn't stop him. He hissed as he ran, knocking me so hard upside my head that I blacked out for a moment.

I came to as Loki neared the trees. That's when my sobs began in earnest. Ull had told me the trees were a transport delineation between this realm and the next—and once we crossed that border, Loki would be able to open a portal and take us to Jotunheim. I had fought and I had failed. My head spun and I saw a terrifying vision of my future.

"Bring me my wife!" Loki's maniacal voice echoed through his castle.

I was forced to my feet by two enormous guards, one dragging me by my elbow and the other prodding me with the flat side of an oversized ice-pick. My wrists were cuffed together and my legs bound with heavy chains. And my outfit . . . even though it couldn't have been more than thirty-degrees indoors, I wore a sleeveless turtleneck dress that barely covered my behind, and four-inch, pointy-toed stilettos.

This was so not the way a lady should be dressed.

The guards shoved me down a narrow hallway made entirely of ice. I skidded in my treacherous footwear and the sharp end of the ice-pick jabbed me in my side. My blood dripped as I walked, leaving a crimson trail of splatters on the glossy ice floor. It was a shame to dirty the hall, but I knew it would be cleaned by the time I reached Loki's chamber. From all appearances, my captor did not tolerate untidiness.

The guard holding my elbow opened the tall ivory door at the end of the hall and shoved me through. I was in Loki's bedchamber now, the dead last place I ever wanted to be. A four-poster bed covered in fur blankets stood in the center of the circular room, and windows framed in thick velvet curtains covered every wall. Loki stood beside an ancient desk, one hand on the ornate chair beside it. He wore a long, black robe and fur boots, and his dark hair was slicked back.

"You are dismissed." Loki waved at his guards and crossed to me. He stroked my cheek with one bony finger, and I turned my head to avoid his touch. Just the sight of him made me want to empty the contents of my stomach all over his pristine ice floor.

"Shall I undo your chains so you can join me in my quarters, wife? Or will you be sleeping in your cell again?"

I lifted my chin. "I'll never be your wife."

"But you already are, poppet," Loki hissed. He grabbed my left hand and thrust it in front of my face. I had no choice but to stare at the grotesque black stone that sat where Ull's exquisite ring had been. "Or don't you remember our special bond?"

"There's no bond, you cretin. I'm Ull's, and nothing will ever change that." I turned on one stilettoed heel and strode toward the door.

"Ah, there's the fighting spirit I so enjoy in my bride." Loki snapped his fingers and I flew unwittingly to his side. It was a dance we'd done every night since my capture, and I knew exactly how it would end: with me chained in the frozen cell adjacent to Loki's bedroom, crying myself to sleep. Remembering my life with Ull gave me the strength to get through every day of this nightmare. I prayed continually for a miracle—some connection to whatever realm Ull was in. But none came.

"I hate you." I struggled against Loki's touch. He wrapped his arms around me and breathed down my neck.

"Ahh, but I'm all you have, sweet Kristia. You may as well resign yourself to your fate. You're never going home. Odin severed Jotunheim from the realms this afternoon."

I gasped. "He wouldn't."

"He did," Loki seethed. "He held off long enough for my army to take down five full units of his warriors, but eventually he had to give up. Severing the realm was the only way to protect his precious Asgard. And Ull? I sent two of my assassins for him at noon. I'm sorry, my pet, he didn't make it."

I sucked in a sharp breath, ignoring the sudden ache in my stomach. There could be no world without Ull—he was my reason for breathing, my absolute everything, and if he didn't exist . . .

A black void filled my gut, rose up my throat, and took over my brain. Everything went dark and the ground dropped out below me. I stumbled, trying to catch my balance. The darkness threatened to overwhelm me, but I fought it off. Ull wouldn't have wanted me to give up. And even though Ull was . . . gone . . . I owed it to our love to make him proud.

"Go to Helheim, Loki." I squared my shoulders and looked Loki in the eye, then I reared my head back and brought it down hard on his collar bone. The crack of its fracture was satisfying enough to ease the pain in my forehead.

"Oh, Kristia." Loki cackled, waving his hand across his chest and healing the break. "Such a shame to dirty that lovely face."

He lifted my chin and I glared at him, blinking the blood out of my eyes. I'd cut myself badly, and now Loki wasn't even injured. Son of a—

"Just embrace your future." Loki swept his arm around the room, bringing it to rest on my waist. "And don't you ever try a stunt like that again." He slapped me hard across the face. My jaw burned, the surface pain distracting me from the black hole of agony swelling in my chest.

"I hate you," I said again, bringing my cuffed hands

as far apart as I could and striking Loki. The chain left a nasty red mark, but Loki waved one finger across his cheek and healed himself.

"And I hate you." Loki brought a fist down on my head, knocking me to the ground. I struck my temple on the arm of the chair as I fell, and waves of nausea overtook me as the room blurred.

"Someone will come," I lisped through semi-consciousness. "Inga or Gunnar—"

"Both dead, my pet. My assassins couldn't leave any witnesses, now, could they? And that old woman? She was the first to go."

Olaug.

I couldn't take it anymore. The ice-covered ground was so cool against my cheek. It soothed my burning flesh. My temple throbbed, my gut ached, and my head felt like it had been pierced with a thousand burning blades. Inga, Gunnar, Olaug. All dead because of me. And Ull . . . my beloved Ull . . .

I gave in to the darkness, not caring that the ice of the floor was burning my skin. I was going to spend an eternity in this desolate wasteland. But whatever the horrors of Jotunheim, being without Ull would be the worst part.

My existence was completely and totally hopeless.

I shook myself out of the vision, my tears falling in torrents. Loki's crazed laughter rang clear as we reached the trees. "Goodbye, my friends!"

As Loki raised his arm to take us to my personal hell, I looked for my husband one last time. *I love you*, I mouthed in his general direction. I couldn't see well enough through my tears to find his face.

As I formed the words, something hard tackled us. It hurt, and I knew Loki had made his escape—Ull had told me transports between the realms could be painful. But when I felt the dirt under my back, and smelled that woodsy scent I was all too familiar with, I knew I was going to be okay.

Until the bleeding began.

"No!" Loki shrieked. "We should be in Jotunheim. Not Asgard!"

"And yet, here you are." Ull's voice came from somewhere nearby. I turned my head and saw him a good twenty yards off, lying face down at the base of a tree. He pawed the ground, struggling to stand. Something had gone horribly wrong in his transport—he could barely move.

"Ull!" I cried out.

While I reached for Ull, Loki scrambled to his feet, stepping hard on my abdomen in the process. All the air expelled from my lungs and I lay on the ground, sucking frantically at the dusty air. Loki kicked my torso with one steel-toed boot, putting a fast end to my pathetic attempt to breathe. I inhaled desperately, but nothing happened—it felt as if there was a giant lead ball blocking my throat. Loki kicked me again and the ball dropped to my stomach, a whole new level of pain, but at least I could breathe. I gulped down air with all the dignity of a wide-mouthed bass. I didn't know when I'd get another chance.

I rolled to my side, clawing at the dirt in an effort to pull myself up. My chest felt like an area rug on cleaning day, but I wasn't going to let this beating be the end of me. Problem was, my legs wouldn't work. They shook as I tried to pull myself up, so I pushed up on one arm and resolved to defend myself from the ground.

As I raised my arm to clothesline his ankle, Loki brought the heel of his boot down on my injured wrist.

"Arugh!" I hadn't meant to cry out, but the pain was too intense. Were there cleats on that thing?

"What. Did. You. Do?" Loki screamed as he ground his heel, flattening my left arm and producing a sickening crack. The bones were shattered, and blood seeped from beneath his boot. When he lifted the heel, a stream of red shot skyward from my wrist. He'd ruptured a major vein.

"Kristia!" Ull's shout rang through the woods.

The trees above me spun in a dizzying pattern. The effect reminded me of the carnival ride Ardis and I took in Seaside during a fifth-grade field trip. She'd gotten sick and lost her ice cream. Being of a stronger constitution, I'd been luckier.

But today was a different story. As the trees tottered dangerously close to my face then rose back to the sky, I leaned over my one good arm and threw up. My stomach heaved, constricting every time I caught sight of the stream of blood shooting from my wrist.

"What's the matter, poppet? Can't handle a little fight? Didn't anybody teach you how?" Loki glared down at me, fire sparking out of his venomous eyes. Specks of my blood covered his right cheek. "So the

172

almighty *human* is a weakling after all. Pity. And I had so looked forward to a fair fight."

He eyed me levelly, then bent to pick something up. My vision blurred and the trees swam closer again. I turned my head to the side. The earth was bathed in a pool of red. I was losing so much blood. And from the feel of it, my consciousness wasn't long for this world. I focused on the trees again—anything to take away the picture of my very essence spurting from my compromised vein. The branches swayed back and forth. The evergreens reminded me of the trees back in Nehalem. They were kind of beautiful. They waved at me, almost like they were trying to speak. *Hello, Kristia. Sorry about the way you're going to die. Guess immortality isn't set in stone, huh?*

No, wait. They were waving forcefully from left to right. Left to right. Left to . . . what was to my right again? I turned to see what they were pointing to and a small smile formed on my lips. Ull was finally on his feet. He shot into the sky like a beautiful airborne superhero, and as he landed in a low crouch a few feet behind Loki he locked eyes with me. I breathed a sigh of relief; Ull was going to be okay. I lost him as my lids lowered, consciousness escaping, and when I managed to lift them again Loki had darted into my line of vision. He held a fractured tree branch just over my heart: the perfect weapon.

"Goodbye, Kristia." He raised his arms and I squeezed my eyes shut, preparing for the blow. In my final moment I sent out one last thought.

I love you, Ull.

CHAPTER FOURTEEN

"NO!" THE AGONIZED CRY filled the clearing. Ull's grief cut to my core, but I couldn't help him. I couldn't help anyone.

I heard the stick connect but I didn't feel the pain. My consciousness floated toward the trees, their rich green needles getting closer with each breath of wind. My arms were limp at my side; my shattered wrist no longer throbbed. My eyes zeroed in on the pale blue of the sky, dotted with cotton-candy clouds. I sucked air deep into my chest and a mist filled my head. It swirled gently, clearing all residual discomfort with my exhale. I felt only peace, calm, and absolute serenity.

But the peace was short-lived.

"No!" Ull's cry broke through my calm. He thundered to my side and dropped to the ground. He ripped the branch from my chest. And he murmured something I couldn't understand.

Then came the pressure. Strong hands pumped the center of my sternum. One, two, three, four, five. Moist lips covered mine and a breath of air inflated my lungs. Another. Then the pressure on my chest bone again. It was uncomfortable. And it pulled my consciousness back into my body, where every nerve was exploding with pain.

"Come on, baby. Stay with me." Ull's voice cracked. He resumed his compressions, this time pumping at double speed. "Do not go anywhere."

"You can't save her." Loki's voice came from my right. "And if you did, I'd just kill her again."

"You," Ull growled. He scooped me up and started to run. I knew he was trying to protect me from the jotun, but the jarring motion awakened the handful of nerve endings that weren't already on fire. I wanted to scream at him to stop moving. But I couldn't even open my mouth.

"You will be safe here." Ull laid me gently on a hard surface.

"Are you sure about that?" Loki called from across the clearing. The earth shook and I used every bit of strength I had to drag one eyelid open. An enormous boulder crashed just two feet east of my face.

"Enough!" Ull stood directly in front of me. He glanced down. His shoulders dropped and his fists unclenched when he took in my partly opened eye. I must have looked like I'd crossed the fighting end of an angry grizzly, but at least I was alive.

I forced my other eye open and saw Ull turning his head from me to Loki and back. He didn't want to leave my side, but Loki would take us both out if Ull didn't stop him first.

"What's the matter, Ull? Asgard's prince too weak to protect himself?" The earth shook again and another boulder landed just in front of Ull. "Those were my warning shots. I won't miss her next time."

Ull's battle cry rang through the woods. He launched himself at Loki, arms outstretched and legs trailing behind. He was fierce. Lethal. And absolutely terrifying.

Loki didn't have time to move before Ull was on top of him. Ull delivered one brutal blow to Loki's head before pulling his arm back and opening his palm. Loki's eyes widened in fear as a beam shot from Ull's hand, and in the next instant, Loki was frozen. I watched him lie on the ground and I waited for his body to go limp. Nothing happened. He was stunned, not dead.

But before Ull delivered his final shot, Loki had gotten one off of his own. As Loki had fallen to the dirt, a spark sailed from his hand to the tree directly above me. It had compromised the tree's stability, and now I heard a loud crack as a heavy limb broke free. I was too weak to move out of its way—I could only watch in horror as it fell.

It took Ull one second to cross the clearing and reach for the branch, but as he caught it the limb managed to hit my abdomen. The air rushed out of my lungs, and a dull ache spread from my stomach to my chest, then settled in my head. I stared at Ull's face, just inches from mine. It was perfect: the strong lines of his jaw, the planes of his cheeks, the absolutely endless blue eyes. The image blurred until there were two Ulls, then they merged back together.

Ull's brows framed that little *V* he so often wore. I tried to reach up to smooth the wrinkle away but I couldn't move my arm. I'd lost massive amounts of blood. Everything hurt so badly. I closed my eyes against the pain. It was too much.

"It will be okay, sweetheart." I felt Ull stroke my hair. "We will make you well."

I opened my eyes a fraction of an inch to look at my love. The dull ache turned to numbness, and within seconds it overtook my entire body. I forced myself to breathe. I only managed two shallow intakes before my lungs gave up.

And then the peace came back.

"No!" One forceful syllable kept me from drifting away. Ull pried my mouth open. Two warm breaths pushed down my throat. Then Ull leaned into my chest, pumping hard. One, two, three . . . My consciousness shifted, and I saw the scene from outside my body. Ull's brow furrowed and his eyes stared unseeingly at the ground. After thirty counts he resumed the breaths. Then pumps. *Breaths. Pumps. Breaths. Pumps.* He broke out in a sweat. The adorable flop of blond hair that normally fell over one eye was so soaked it stuck to his forehead. *Breaths. Pumps. Breaths. Pumps.* The cycle went on and on. He should have been exhausted, but the more time that passed the more frantic he became.

It's okay. Let me go.

The gut-wrenching sob tore at my soul. Ull wept. I could see each individual tear falling from his eyes. They came slowly at first, each easily distinguished from the others, but soon they flowed in a torrent, binding together in a shimmery mist. The mist began to sparkle, and it moved toward my body, sealing me in a luminous shell. Ull's shoulders shook. He hunched over my torso in a heartbreaking display. He lifted my head into his lap, cradling me in his forearms and kissing my forehead, as if sheer willpower could bring me back.

Oh, Ull.

I wanted to touch him, to comfort him. To let him know I wasn't hurting, that it would all be okay. But I didn't know that. What would happen to our family? Ardis? Inga and Gunnar? Had Tyr and Odin stopped the ship? Were our realms on a collision course set for complete and total destruction?

"Kristia," Ull moaned as he squeezed my shoulders. "Baby." Each syllable came as a gasp. Ull's silvery tears now encased my entire corpse—he must have cried a full gallon of them.

As I marveled at my poor husband's shimmering tears, they started to vibrate. Slowly at first, and then with the speed of one of Inga's beloved racecars, they shook just above my skin. My fingers and toes tingled as the tears started to bounce off each other like drops of water on a hot skillet. My arms and legs regained feeling, and warmth filled my chest. The sparkling liquid continued its dance until the warmth spread from the top of my head all the way down to my feet, and it leaped off my body and pooled onto the ground just as I drew an enormous breath.

"Kristia!"

I heard Ull's joyful shout before I could exhale. He cradled me and pressed warm kisses to my forehead and cheeks before claiming my mouth.

"Oh, sweetheart!" He pulled me to his chest so tight I could feel his heart beating. The rapid thrumming betrayed the terror he must have felt. "I thought you left me."

He lowered his head to mine again, crushing my lips against his. His tongue parted my lips almost forcefully, and as he pushed against me I melted into his embrace. How could he think I would willingly go anywhere without him?

"Ull," I murmured. I ran my fingers through his hair, pushing the sopping strands off his sweat-stained forehead. "I love you so much."

I felt an ache in my left wrist but I didn't care. I pulled Ull close again and he kissed me with abandon, seeming to forget that I was battered, bruised, and had recently been staked by a madman. He rolled so he hovered lightly over my torso.

"Do not ever leave me again." It was an order, and I nodded weakly.

"Okay."

I reached up with my good arm and pulled him on top of me. The weight of the enormous god resting directly on my injuries hurt like the dickens, but I was too relieved to think straight. All I could register was the feel of Ull's lips, his body on mine, and the absolutely heavenly smell that was my husband.

Until I heard the pop.

"Ull?" I looked up.

"Run. Now!" He jumped to his feet and lifted me alongside him. He pointed me away from the trees and gave a shove that sent me stumbling across the clearing. When he saw me safely sprawled at the base of a boulder, Ull charged in the opposite direction.

It took me a moment to clear the ringing from my ears, and by the time I could stand unsupported, the battle was underway. Ull's stunning spell had worn off and Loki was on the attack. The two gods were only forty yards away from my rock shelter—far enough that I was safe from the flying fists, but near enough that I could hear every sickening blow. Loki wrenched his bicep out of Ull's grasp and darted to the base of an evergreen. Ull pivoted to face his foe, lowered his head, and charged. He threw himself at Loki.

I'd never seen anything like it. They were unmatched physically, Loki tall and wiry, and Ull taller and brawnier. If it had been a fistfight the outcome would have been clear, but while Ull came at Loki with physical attacks, Loki responded by casting spells. They sent Ull reeling as no punch from Loki's thin frame could. My heart lurched each time he was struck. Seeing Ull under fire tore at my soul.

I knew that Ull was just as skilled a magician as Loki, probably more so, but his anger marred any logical attack. He charged again, a terrifying battle cry erupting from his throat, barreling down on the half-jotun like a bull in a fight. It might have been beautiful if it weren't so scary. Loki's eyes betrayed his fear, but he muttered an incantation and with a wave of his arms sent Ull flying high in the air, legs flailing, before a sturdy tree stopped his trajectory. The tree cracked and fell to the ground but Ull landed on his feet unscathed. Anger seethed from every inch of his magnificent being and he lowered his head to attack.

"Are you all right, Kristia?" For the first time I realized I wasn't alone in my corner of the woods.

"Sif?" I looked around, wondering just how many of my brain cells had been sacrificed in my brush with death. "I thought you were fighting the wolf and the snake."

"I am trying." Sif gritted her teeth. "But it has not been going so well since Odin called for Thor. We thought this would be such an easy fight; that one of us could handle it. We were wrong." Greenish-blue bruises marred her otherwise perfect body. She looked as if she'd had a run-in with the wrong end of a hungry mountain lion.

"What? Thor isn't here?" I looked around and saw we were in a familiar landscape. The English lavender was missing, but in every other way it was the battlefield from my nightmares. The place I'd been killed a thousand different ways by two terrifying monsters. Oh, jeez. How many times was I going to have to cheat death today?

"Sif? Are we in Asgard's battlefield?"

"We are. You. Me. My son. That monster Loki." She jutted her chin to her right. "And a giant wolf and serpent who have been playing cat and mouse with me all afternoon."

"You haven't killed them yet." My heart sank.

"No. And I only have the one sword, so there's not much I can ask you to do to help me." She squinted. I followed her sightline and my insides churned. My breath came in jagged gasps as I saw the demons circling in the distance, making their way toward us. "The best you can do is stay behind me and hope they do not attack from opposite sides."

"I can do more than that." I spoke through gritted teeth. Planting myself a few feet away from my mother-in-law, I held my fingers together and closed my eyes. An uncomfortable pressure built behind my lids as I sent my energy to the center of my frontal lobe. Ignoring the pain, I pushed the pressure down my neck, along my arm and to my fingertips. They began to burn from the cold, and when I opened my eyes a blue cloud swirled against my palm. With more care than I'd ever exercised, I opened my fingers. I had one, maybe two shots at slowing these things down, and misfiring was *not* an option.

The wolf lunged toward Sif and I raised my palm. With a vicious swipe I sent a stream hurtling in front of the animal. An icy surface covered the ground, and Fenrir skidded on four paws. He slid across the surface, totally out of control, and slammed into a nearby tree.

"Did you do that?" Sif turned to me.

"Yeah. Ull showed me on our honeymoon."

Sif hid a smile. "I do hope you are able to teach him to relax. Eventually."

I closed my eyes and turned toward the snake. "I'm working on it."

A low hiss alerted me to the snake's movement, so I directed another ice field at the ground, hoping to slow its trajectory. When I opened my eyes, the oversized reptile was moving calmly across the frozen surface while Fenrir stalked across his own ice block with cat-like reflexes. Somehow I'd forgotten their father was part jotun. With frost giant genes, a little winter weather pattern might take them by surprise, but it wasn't going to deter them for long.

While I regrouped, I whipped my arm around my head. A blizzard whirled toward the demonic duo. They pushed through, gaining traction as they moved. A hailstorm followed, earning no more than a mocking snarl. When my pathetic attempt to summon lightning proved useless, I had to admit defeat.

This wasn't working.

Ull had taught me to assess my surroundings. There weren't any conventional weapons lying around, and the wolf had already halved the distance between us. I couldn't see the snake anymore, but I knew he was en route. Not far away, Loki was mounting roundhouse kicks to Ull's jaw. The scene shifted to a slightly darker red and I used my right hand to grab the only thing I could find. It was a stick, three feet in length and six inches in diameter, with a sharply pointed end. It looked vaguely familiar; it would have to do.

I thought back to the lesson Ull gave me on our honeymoon. *If I ever found myself without a weapon, a ninety-degree strike with a broken branch would give me enough time to run.* But I wasn't running.

"Let's end this."

CHAPTER FIFTEEN

I NARROWED MY EYES and stood against Sif so we were back to back, slowly pivoting to fully assess the field. Suddenly she yelled out, a guttural cry that emanated from deep in her chest. I permitted myself one brief glance and saw her running full bore toward the enormous wolf. She leapt to meet him midair, sword drawn at the ready. I heard the horrifying sound of claws and metal tearing flesh and fur, but I didn't get to see what happened after that because I was under siege.

My heart thudded against my ribcage, sending adrenaline coarsing through my veins. Fear roared between my ears as I realized the snake had found me. Its oversized trunk wound its way through the dirt and rocks until the animal came to rest just beyond my reach. Beady red eyes assessed their target, and a faint hiss escaped slanted nostrils. I stabbed, but it rose to stand on its tail just outside the radius of my crude weapon. I stabbed again, realizing with alarm that the snake was at least eleven feet tall and measured a full four feet in diameter. It was even bigger than it had been in my nightmares.

I took a step back to reassess and the snake struck. It lunged for my feet and I jumped. The red eyes focused and it struck again, this time catching me on the ankle and piercing my leg with venomous fangs. My calf felt like it had burst into flames. Poison ebbed from the snake, making its way up my leg and taking root in my blood stream. I shifted my weight onto one foot, willing myself not to cry out. I narrowed my eyes as the snake struck again, this time aiming for my torso. Pounding fists on fur sounded behind me, and I knew Sif was locked in her own life or death battle. Raising the stick as high as my mangled hand would allow, I jumped out of the snake's path and forced my stake into the creature's trajectory. It met its target at just the right moment, driving all the way through the serpent's leathery skin. The snake paused mid-strike, its reptilian features frozen in shock. It fell to my feet with a thud, and I kicked it fiercely, stomping on its head for good measure. The crack of its skull was music to my ears.

I turned to find my mother-in-law standing atop her own captive, and I averted my eyes just before I heard the piercing of metal on flesh. There was a groan, then a gurgling, and when I glanced up, Sif withdrew her sword from the wolf's chest.

The monsters from my nightmares would never bother me again.

Though I saw Sif wilt with exhaustion, I knew I was needed elsewhere. I turned my focus to my husband, who was locked in battle. Ull had been holding his own, but Loki now had the upper hand. Loki threw uppercuts at my beloved's perfect jaw, and my world turned even redder.

It was time to cancel Loki's birth certificate.

The numbness in my compromised leg wasn't going to stop me. I shifted my weight and tugged at the stake firmly lodged in my attacker. As I tried to free it, I heard a *pop* from the far end of the field. Gunnar landed in the trees, crossbow in hand, and ran for Loki at full hilt. Loki waved his hand at Ull and sent him flying. He struck a tree and fell to the ground, then sat up slowly, cupping his jaw in one hand.

"Ull!" I shrieked. My heart pounded frantically as I watched red liquid course through his fingers, dripping in a pool on the dirt. He was losing blood, and though he waved his free hand at the wound, his magic was taking its sweet time; he'd been badly hurt. Gunnar growled at Loki and fired off three arrows in quick succession, but Loki's footwork was fast and he evaded the onslaught. Gunnar circled, stalking Loki as he backed away, then aimed his crossbow and shot again.

Loki conjured up a sword and flung himself at Gunnar. Gunnar spun out of the way, and Loki flew past, landing face-first in the dirt. He jumped up as Gunnar approached from behind, but he wasn't fast enough. Before Loki could turn around, Gunnar nailed him in the back of the head, first with his crossbow, then with his fist.

Gunnar drew an arrow and took aim but Loki laced his sword through the weapon and ripped it from Gunnar's grasp. He delivered a swift knee to Gunnar's groin before throwing him into a rock. Gunnar bounced off the hard surface and onto the dirt, doubled over in the fetal position. He held his hands between his legs as he let out a loud groan. The sound of pain echoed through the clearing. After a few seconds, Gunnar rolled onto his back and stared at the clouds. If his unfocused gaze was any indication, he was massively disoriented.

I was afraid for him, but Loki must have decided he wasn't a threat anymore—he turned his attention back to Ull.

I held my breath. Ull was back on his feet, charging at Loki. The jotun cackled as a demonic half-smile lit up his horrible features. As Ull leapt to pounce, Loki met him midair, their bodies colliding with a thunderous clap. They fell to the ground, exchanging blows so forceful it sounded like a storm was rolling in.

Ull pinned Loki beneath him and let out a roar. Rage filled his eyes and he swung punch after punch at Loki's head. I heard the now-too-familiar crunch of breaking bones and watched Ull's tremendous biceps flex as he relentlessly punished my attacker.

Then the battle took a turn.

Ull swung at Loki's face, breaking the jaw and leaving a trail of blood on his fist. Loki returned the punch with a kick to Ull's shin, making Ull cry out. Ull drove a knee into Loki's torso, and Loki emptied the contents of his stomach in a thick brown stream. The next second he drew himself up and swiftly kicked Ull's chest. Ull was left heaving on his knees, gasping for breath.

Loki paused, having momentarily gained control. Ull was trying so hard to reorient himself, he didn't realize Loki now crossed behind him. Loki raised a hand to deliver the ending blow, and the scene shifted to a dark crimson.

I was furious. Balder was dead. Sif and Gunnar were barely breathing. And now Loki wanted to kill the only man I'd ever loved.

A girl can only take so much.

I twisted the stick protruding from the snake and pulled until it was free. My left hand was still bleeding, but it was strong enough to hold the stick steady, so long as I controlled it with my right.

Loki's back was to me. His fists hovered over Ull's head.

I ignored the blinding pain in my poisoned leg and took off at a full sprint. Loki didn't even notice when I started running toward him—I'm not sure he could have. I thought I'd run fast on Asgard Cay, but that was a Fun Run compared to the power building in my legs now. I pushed off the ground, picking up speed with each step. The earth flew under my feet, the field blurring as I advanced on my target.

I was about to knock Loki into the middle of next week looking both ways for Sunday.

"Nobody," I breathed as I ran. "Hurts." I was closer

now. "My." I raised the stick over my head. "Husband!"

I screamed as I thrust the stick through Loki's ribcage with all the force I had left. It pierced his thick skin all the way through, stopping only when my hands came to rest against his spine. I released the stick but it didn't budge.

Loki turned, his eyes wide with shock. A full foot of wood protruded from his chest, which was quickly turning scarlet. Blood seeped from the wound, covering his torso in its sticky film. His eyes bulged and his fave visibly paled as he glanced down.

"You," he growled. "Die already."

"Fat chance."

He lunged at me, but he didn't have the strength to make contact. He just fell forward, un-impaling himself as the impact drove the stick back out of his body. And he didn't move again. His body was limp on the ground, face-first in a pile of his own blood.

Ull knelt a few feet away. He'd taken in this last bit with hooded eyes. He shakily drew himself up to his full height, muscles still flexed for battle. Drawing a circle in the air with one finger, he conjured a silvery bubble. It lowered onto Loki's body, trapping the lifeless creature within its skin. Ull raised the bubble with a finger so it was suspended several feet above the ground. At this, Ull's body sagged. Mine did too. His eyes found me, profound relief evident in his gaze. I nodded in agreement. He looked to Gunnar, who was getting unsteadily to his feet.

"You all right, man?" Ull asked. He lifted his shirt to wipe the blood off his jaw, affording me a glimpse of his spectacular abdomen. My pulse quickened.

"That was some fight." Gunnar rubbed his wrists. Ugly bruises covered his arms. "It's been a while, eh?"

"I think we are getting older." Ull lowered his shirt and rolled his shoulders back.

"Indeed."

"Mother?" Ull called across the field. Sif pushed herself to her feet.

"I am all right, son. Thanks to your wife." She shot me a weary smile. "I could not handle them both on my own."

Ull crossed the clearing in ten long strides. When he reached my side, he tenderly stroked my now-discolored leg. The pain began to ease immediately, and I knew he was working his special brand of magic to eradicate the snake's poison.

"You were incredible." He treated me to the rakish smile I'd first fallen in love with. "I have never seen anything like that in all of my years. You truly are . . ." He shook his head.

My breath caught as he slowly lowered himself on one knee, taking both of my hands and kissing them softly. He bowed his head.

"Your Grace." He threw my long-ago words back at me.

"Stop it." My cheeks flamed.

"I mean it, Kristia; you saved my life. And my mother's. And probably Gunnar's, too. You said all along the prophecy was not law—that we could write our own fate. I did not believe it. But you did the impossible. You altered our destiny."

"*We* altered our destiny. You saved my life first." I pulled him up so we stood eye to eye. Well, eye to chest, but I craned my neck to look into the baby blues that held my heart.

My knees buckled. Ull caught me easily, one arm wrapping around my waist and pulling me so my chest was pressed against him. He leaned down, dipping me so low my head tipped back. I felt cool breath at my neck, then the tip of his nose running along the ridge of my jaw. I shivered. His hand cradled my head and he lifted me slightly, bringing my face to his.

"Kristia," he exhaled.

"Mmm." It was the best I could do. He'd wiped my brain clear of all cohesive thought.

"I love you." And just like that his touch went from cool to hot. He brought his lips to mine with a force I wasn't expecting. One hand grabbed at my hair while the other crushed me to him, his enormous palm flat against my shoulder blades. My skin burned and I dug my nails into the muscles of his back, desperate to close even the smallest gap between us. Ull's hand dropped to my lower back—now he fully supported my weight. I fought to breathe as his mouth moved to my jaw, then the hollow of my neck.

"Ull," I moaned softly.

"Guys." Gunnar cleared his throat. I'd forgotten he was there. I tried to right myself, but Ull wasn't letting me move.

"What?" Ull hissed. He gave Gunnar what could only be described as the stink-eye.

"Sif is right there. She's staring at you." She was.

192

Ull's mom was just across the clearing, doing her best to hide her smile.

"So?" Ull seemed unbothered, but eventually he had to give in to my squirming. "Oh, all right, darling."

He set me on my feet before he glanced down.

"Look at your hand. You are hurting." He kissed the wounds softly, murmuring something I couldn't understand. The blood stopped. I watched in awe as the cuts healed themselves. As long as I lived, I'd never get used to that particular talent. Ull wrapped his arms around me, careful not to agitate the bruises he hadn't yet assessed. But the precaution was unnecessary. My pain was gone.

The day caught up with me. Breathing in his familiar scent, I started to cry. The tears came slowly at first, and then heavy sobs consumed my body and I wept terribly in Ull's arms. The enormity of what it would have meant to be separated from him for all time hit like a logging truck with busted breaks. Ull held me until my tears slowed and my sobs were reduced to pitiful hiccups. He stroked my hair, gently picking the leaves from its tangled mess. When I collected myself enough to look at his face, it held such tenderness that I nearly started crying all over again.

I clung to his chest—I'd almost lost him forever. His gentle murmurs and soft kisses reduced the hiccups to sniffles, and I focused on keeping myself very still until my eyes cleared.

"I was so afraid I was going to lose you," I whispered. "I never should have left Ýdalir."

"Shh," Ull soothed. "You will never be without me.

You, my dear, are stuck with me." He held up his ring finger. "No take-backs, remember?"

"Is Ardis okay?" I asked timidly.

"She's fine," Gunnar told me, closing his mobile phone and ending a conversation I hadn't realized was happening. "She's actually safe in New York. Inga just checked on her. What you saw was an illusion."

I hung my head. I still had so much to learn.

"Do not feel bad. Loki is a terribly powerful magician. He is much more skilled than I am. Any one of us could have been deceived." Ull pulled my hands from my face, looking me in the eye. "But please do not ever leave my side again. I need you with me, always."

"Always." Forgetting that his mom was in the clearing, I reached up to kiss Ull's perfect mouth. I curled under his arm, molding myself to the muscles of his torso. He rested his cheek on my head. He must have been exhausted.

"Is Loki dead?" I asked quietly.

"Unfortunately, no. It takes more than that to kill a god." Tell me about it.

"But he nearly killed me. How?"

"We have a bit of an Achilles heel in our left wrists—the vein that runs from our fourth finger to our heart can be compromised."

"He pierced my vein," I whispered.

"But you survived. Thank Odin." Ull kissed the top of my head.

"You fought hard, Kristia." Gunnar threw his crossbow over his shoulder and grinned. "Good work."

"You have never been more beautiful to me." Ull's

look made me blush, though I wasn't about to object to the way he placed his hands on my hips.

"Is Loki going to attack us again?"

"I doubt it. He will not wake up any time soon. And when he does, there is no way, magic or no, he could possibly escape that bubble. It is an Asgardian prison cell. Odin will put Loki on trial for his crimes, and in all likelihood he will receive a life sentence. Asgard willing, we will never have to worry about him again."

Sif dusted herself off and began to cross the clearing. "If I have anything to say about it, that monster will be locked up into perpetuity."

"Locked up? No. Ull, we have to kill him right now. If we don't, Olaug will die. He cast the Crushing Curse, remember?"

"You think killing him will end the curse?" Ull asked.

"When I was in the tenth realm, Loki said the only way to break the curse was to kill him, or find some secret artifact nobody can find."

"The Healing Stone?" Gunnar rubbed his neck. "Nobody's seen that for years."

"We have to save Olaug."

"We all agree on that." Sif nodded as she reached us.

"We cannot kill Loki ourselves. I would if I could. Nobody has more reason than I do to want him dead." Ull's eyes blazed.

"Then why can't we kill him?"

"It is a physical impossibility—at least for me. Loki protects himself with magic so strong, not even Odin can unbind it. It is remarkable you were able to incapacitate him so fully. You are much more powerful than you give yourself credit for." He stroked the small of my back and a tremor ran up my spine.

"So how do we help Olaug?"

"Well, I wager debilitating Loki will have slowed the curse significantly. A curse is only as powerful as the one who casts it, and if Loki is suspended in unconsciousness, then his curse will reflect that."

"He predicted her death in two days."

"That will not be possible. He is too weak for the curse to follow through to completion. But it may linger in her spirit. She may feel some residual effects."

"So how do we cure her?"

"So long as Loki is incarcerated, his curse will be frozen. But if for some reason Odin delivers less than a life sentence, then we would need to find the stone." Ull pulled me close. "Do not worry yourself, darling. One way or another, we will take care of Olaug. I promise you."

I rested my head on his shoulder, too exhausted to do much more. "How'd we end up in Asgard anyway? I had a vision of Jotunheim."

Ull twirled his finger in the air. "I could not stop the transport, but what kind of magician would I be if I did not at least throw in a detour?"

"What about Thor and Odin? Are they okay?"

Gunnar grimaced. "I don't know. Inga hasn't heard anything, and Olaug isn't back from Asgard yet. We have to wait."

"I will return to Odin's hall to see what more I can do." Sif squeezed Ull's arm, and turned to leave.

"Sif, you need to rest," I argued.

"Not if Thor needs me." Her face was grim as she raced through the forest.

"Will she be okay? Shouldn't she take the Bifrost or something?"

"My mother can handle anything. And Odin's hall is only twenty miles away. It will only take her a few minutes on foot; no need for magic."

"Right."

Just then, two warriors emerged from the trees. Ull instructed them to take Loki's body to Heimdall. I heard them mutter the oath before Heimdall opened the Bifrost into the clearing, and the two warriors and the disgraced half-jotun disappeared from my sight.

"Heimdall's more than twenty miles away, huh?" I pointed to the dust left in the Bifrost's wake.

"Protocol," Ull explained. "Prisoners require armed Bifrost transports. No exceptions."

I breathed a heavy sigh, exhaustion overcoming me. My limbs could have been made of lead; each movement took what felt like an overwhelming amount of energy. Ull supported my weight as we made our way toward the portal Loki had used to bring us from Ýdalir.

"Sorry, Gunnar," I said with a sideways glance. "I didn't mean to get you into a fight."

Gunnar waved a hand at me. "Shoot, Kristia. It's been way too long since Ull and I did something like that. It was great." He chucked me gently on the arm.

At the portal Ull instructed me to hold on to him and close my eyes until we got back to Bibury. "This will not feel good."

He wasn't kidding. By the time we'd reached the pasture behind Ýdalir I was bent over and barely retaining the contents of my stomach.

"It does get easier, love. Each transport is less painful, I promise." Ull stroked my hair as I stood.

"Can't wait," I muttered.

When we reached the cottage, Inga ran out. She jumped into Gunnar's arms and pelted him with kisses. He winced at the sudden contact and she leaned back, taking in his bruises.

"Oh baby, you're hurt." Inga touched Gunnar's bicep with the back of one finger.

"I'm almost healed, don't worry about it." Gunnar leaned to kiss her again but she held up her hand.

"Nonsense. The ones on your arm are still green. Ull. Fix him." She set her stare on Ull.

"*Vær så snill,*" Ull reminded her. "You didn't say please."

"Fix him, Myhr." Inga didn't blink. "*Vær så snill.*"

"As you wish." Ull waved his hand at Gunnar, and the bruises disappeared. "All better now?"

"I was nearly better before. But thanks anyway, mate." Gunnar laughed, and pulled Inga close. He dipped her low to the ground and planted a solid kiss on her lips. "Missed you, doll."

"Me too." She gazed adoringly at him as he set her on her feet. Then she tugged on his hand and beamed at me. "Come on. There's food inside. You'll all feel better after you eat."

We followed her into the house, where the kitchen counter held plates full of fresh apple turnovers. We helped ourselves to the pastries and I began to feel physically better immediately, though whether from eating the apples or from being back home, I couldn't say. Inside, however, I was a ball of anxiety. We still didn't know how the rest of our family had fared.

But when Olaug finally arrived, her jubilant smile said it all.

"They have done it. Tyr redirected Thor and the Valkyries to disable the ship. The beasts are dead. Heimdall took Loki to the prison chamber to await trial. Ragnarok is over. We have won!"

Inga jumped up and threw herself at Gunnar at the same time Ull swept me into his arms. Twirling me joyfully, he gave me a very thorough kiss. My fingers curled into his thick hair, pulling him closer as I breathed in that woodsy scent. A low rumble built in his chest and he was the first to break our embrace.

Looking to his friends, he said, "Gunnar, Inga, please make yourselves at home. You know where the guest room is. Olaug, thank you for everything you have done for us today. As always, we would have been completely lost without you. But if you will all excuse me." Ull turned for our bedroom, holding me tight in his arms. "I need to be alone with my wife."

The celebration continued behind us, as he whisked me off to our peaceful sanctuary. And I finally accepted that I got to keep this glorious man for my own ever, ever after.

CHAPTER SIXTEEN

IN THE MORNING, ÝDALIR was filled with the scent of fresh apple pastries. I opened my eyes and laid my head on Ull's bare chest. It rose softly with each breath, and I listened to the restful sound, feeling more relaxed than had in days. It was finally over. Loki was locked away; Jotunheim was severed from the realms; the ship was in splinters at the ocean's floor, and the serpent and wolf were dead. Nothing stood in the way of our happily ever after.

I let out a contented sigh, and Ull stirred softly beneath me. One arm looped slowly across my waist, a thumb stroking the small of my back in lazy circles.

"Mmm," Ull murmured. "*God morgen*, Mrs. Myhr."

My stomach fluttered eagerly. *Good morning, indeed.* I lifted my head, and his impish smile confirmed my hopeful suspicions. Ull kissed me soundly, just as Olaug's cheerful voice interrupted from the kitchen.

"Breakfast is ready!" She bellowed, much to my annoyance and Ull's laughter. I hastily threw on fitted jeans and my favorite ballet sweater. We made our way to the kitchen, where the atmosphere was jubilant.

I pulled Olaug aside. "How are you feeling?"

"Better than I have in days. Whatever you did to Loki seems to have worked—I feel practically as good as my old self."

"I'm so glad." I hugged her. "But I have a confession: I told Ull about your condition. I had to. He says you'll improve with Loki all out of sorts like this, and so long as Loki stays in jail, the curse will freeze. But if he's ever released, Ull and I are going to track down that lost artifact to heal you."

Olaug shook her head. "Nobody knows where it is."

"One way or another, we're going to get this thing out of you. I promise."

"I have no doubt, Granddaughter. Now go. Eat." She gestured to the counter with crinkles in the corners of her eyes.

I needed no further invitation. Olaug's fresh apple tarts smelled delicious. I handed one to Ull as I bit into another. The light pastry melted in my mouth; I was ravenous. I joined Gunnar at the kitchen island, clamoring for the freshest batch.

It was this gluttonous sight that greeted Inga when she walked into the room. I stood up, my mouth still covered with pastry crumbs, and walked over to hug my friend. Ull followed, a tart in each hand.

"Great job yesterday, Kristia." Gunnar came over and wrapped an arm around Inga. "I'm sure glad Ull decided to get over himself and start dating you."

"Me, too." I pushed Ull lightly in the arm. "See? All that worrying for nothing."

"My love, I do not think I will ever stop worrying about you. But now I know you are capable of handling yourself." My legs turned to jelly as he kissed me.

"Actually, Kristia, I have a message for you. You have been called to Asgard. Odin wants to thank you." Inga bounced on her toes. A personal summons from Odin was a big deal.

I leaned on Ull.

He smiled. "Asgard owes much to you. Come."

"Shouldn't I change?" I glanced at my outfit self-consciously. A formal visit to Asgard should warrant more than a wrap sweater and denim, though I doubted I had anything fancy enough in my closet to wear to Odin's pad. When I'd been kidnapped by the jotun and ported to Ull's home realm, I hadn't been terribly concerned with my appearance. But now that I'd be going at Odin's invitation . . . well, was pretty sure this was a situation in which Mormor would have advised looking my best.

"Nope." Inga gestured to her own ensemble. She wore slim jeans and a cardigan with her flats. "Asgard is strictly come-as-you-are."

"Whatever you say."

"You look beautiful, darling." I shot Ull a grateful glance.

We gathered in the chamber, a snug fit for five. Ull spoke the oath and the Bifrost opened. This was even more uncomfortable than yesterday's portal transports—it felt as if my bones were sucked up and my skin followed a few seconds behind. My head spun, but before I could pass out, my feet touched a smooth surface. A brightly-colored rainbow wove under my feet. It stretched across the sky, ending at a towering castle growing out of the clouds, brilliant white in the soft pink light. Golden turrets rose from the castle, and shimmering lakes rested at symmetrical intervals around its base. Lofty trees provided shade, their leaves blowing lightly in the soft breeze. Paddleboats were moored at small wooden docks. It was peaceful, pristine, and perfect.

Asgard.

I took it in slowly. Ull squeezed my hand. "Are you ready?"

At my nod, he led our group across the bridge. Ull walked half a step ahead as I looked around in awe. When we reached the castle, a huge man I assumed was Heimdall opened the outer door, ushering us inside. We walked up the steps to a golden inner door. It opened on its own to reveal an enormous hall, filled to capacity. The peaked ceiling bore arches of gold, crossing majestically from one end to the other. Brilliant light streamed from sparkling windows, showering the hall with pearls of luminescence.

The hall fell silent when we stepped inside. I looked up the long aisle and saw Odin in ivory robes sitting on a great throne, Frigga at his side. The room and its occupants were almost blindingly beautiful.

I clung to Ull's arm.

Ull strode up the aisle with the confidence of someone who had walked this path many times. Gunnar and Inga walked calmly behind us with Olaug bringing up the rear. The congregation was silent and still. When we reached Odin, Ull bowed deeply and I followed. At least I hadn't tripped on my way in. This graceful goddess thing was working out for me.

"My fellow Asgardians," Odin began in a deep voice that echoed off the walls. "As you know, last night we undertook the greatest battle in our history. But thanks to the unique talents of our newest member, we emerged victorious. Jotunheim is severed from the realms. Fenrir and the serpent are slain. Loki is in prison. And Asgard remains at peace."

The hall erupted in cheers. I looked at the faces staring up at us, some weary from the weeks of planning, some worse for wear from the covert missions they had carried out in the night, but all triumphant at our collective successes. Odin raised a hand and the crowd quieted.

"Many years ago I asked my grandson to take over for me as Ruler of Asgard. He declined, opting instead to spend his time on Midgard. I did not understand why he was drawn to that realm.

"Ull took a human bride, a woman named Kristia, who showed her character by joining our ranks even when Ull made her aware of the certain death awaiting us all. She became both wife and goddess, and since her ascension she has given us a remarkable gift. She saw our enemies draw their battle plans, and she saw when those plans were changed at the eleventh hour. Though mostly untrained in battle, she fought to protect our realm. Kristia, Goddess of Winter. Please step forward."

I glanced at Ull and he squeezed my hand, nodding toward his grandfather. I prayed I wouldn't fall while walking up the steps.

"Kristia Myhr. You selflessly risked your own future to save ours, and Asgard is eternally in your debt." Odin held out a small, golden key, placing it carefully in my hands. "You are henceforth granted full rights and access to Asgard, as is any true protector of the realm. Use it well, and know that wherever you go, we are with you."

I bowed and the crowd erupted. As they celebrated, Odin leaned in to me. He winked. "Welcome to The Firm."

My brow furrowed. How did he know about Ull's private nickname for his family? Odin smiled mysteriously and sat back in his chair. He patted Frigga's knee and beamed at his people.

I tucked the key safely in my pocket. Ull took my hand and we stood facing the congregation. Olaug, Gunnar, and Inga flanked us, receiving hearty pats on the back from Thor and kisses on each cheek from Sif. My eyes scanned the crowd and I noticed the handsome sandy-haired god who took down the terrible ship leaning against the back wall. He winked at me. I raised my free hand in a wave, and Tyr offered a smirk and a salute. He had the same cheekiness to his smile that Ull got when he was about to do something naughty. As I giggled, Inga let out a squeal.

"Gunnar! Look who's here!" Inga pointed to the god standing next to Tyr. He had the impish eyes and irrestible dimple of another god I knew. In fact, the likeness was uncanny. *Shut the front door.* Did Gunnar have a brother?

Gunnar followed Inga's gaze. When he spotted his doppleganger, his face broke into a grin. "Well look who Freya's cats dragged in." He took off across the room, weaving his way through the sea of gods, and clapped the mystery man on the back.

"Inga," I whispered. "Who is that?"

"Gunnar's brother. We haven't seen him in *forever*. He's all kinds of fabulous." She waved at her brother-in-law and he returned the gesture. Tyr tilted his head toward the door, and Gunnar's brother nodded. He cuffed Gunnar on the shoulder, before ducking out the back door with Tyr. I wondered what, or *who*, was waiting on them.

I looked across the vast crowd, knowing I would have an eternity to get to know each and every Asgardian. But there was only one I wanted to be with right now. I rested my head on Ull's chest as the celebration wound down. Odin dismissed the masses and retreated from the Great Hall. The rest of the party followed suit.

Though I dutifully fell in step after our friends, Ull had other plans. "Come, sweetheart. I have something to show you." He whisked me out a side door, pulling me until we were out of sight and lifting me in his powerful embrace. He carried me to a plush, green meadow at the edge of a lake. A blue gingham picnic blanket was nestled beneath the shade of a willow tree. Wildflowers grew in patches around the meadow, and the sun shone softly from between the silvery willow leaves. It was etherally beautiful at the same time it was altogether familiar. My brain swam, trying to commit each spectacular image to memory, while my heart swelled with the overwhelming realization that I belonged here.

I was Kristia Myhr, Goddess of Winter. And this was my new realm. *Holy cow.*

"When did you have time to set up a picnic?" I asked.

Ull carefully set me down on the blanket and pulled a bottle of champagne from the silver bucket on the grass. "Remember those Valkyries Freya keeps on call for the royal bloodline? I texted one before we crossed the Bifrost; asked her to arrange a little celebration to mark your first official visit to our realm."

"Right. I forgot about them."

Ull uncorked the bottle, poured two glasses, and held one out for me. It was made of the most exquisite crystal, its intricate snowflake pattern reflecting hundreds of rainbows in the filtered sunlight. Ull touched his glass to mine, producing a melodic *clink*, and said simply, "*Skål*, my love."

We drank, staring into the still blue waters of the pond before us. A ripple ran through it as a pair of ivory swans swam slowly across. We watched them paddle motionlessly across the surface.

"Will I ever get used to all of this?" I gestured to Asgard, the meadow, the ponds, the intimate gardens I could see in the distance, the castle seeming to rise out of the clouds.

"Yes and no. Its beauty still catches my breath, after many years. But truthfully, I am most at peace at Ýdalir. It is my home, even though it is a great distance from where I was born to be." He looked at me for a long moment. "Kristia, when we return to Odin he will invite us to live in Asgard. He has decided to let us choose whether to return to Midgard or take up residence here. If living in Asgard will make you happy, then we can set up our home just over the hillside. It is a lovely place to be, and I am sure you will enjoy living here."

"But you won't." I wasn't asking. "Ull, I only want to be where you are. I don't care where we live. Asgard is amazing—I'm sure we'll have great visits here. But we've built our life together at Ýdalir. It's our home, and it's where I want to stay." I hesitated. "Unless you'd rather move . . ." But I didn't have to finish the sentence before I saw the relief in Ull's eyes.

"Not at all. Asgard is wonderful, don't get me wrong, but it is . . . well, a bit much for me. I like country life in Bibury. And taking in the city when we are in London. I would love to spend our newlywed years in Midgard if you would."

"I think that sounds perfect." I clinked his glass with mine, imagining the adventures awaiting us back home. I was sure that between London and Bibury, we would have plenty of distractions to keep us occupied for a few years at least. And after that, who knew? If there was one thing meeting Ull had taught me, it was that I should never try to predict what life held next.

I played with the hammer necklace I still wore and my mind went blank. I plunged easily into a vision of the future. Ull and I, sitting on the grass beneath the shade of the big tree at Ýdalir, a beautiful baby boy nestled in a plush white blanket between us. He kicked his chunky legs in the air, bare toes wiggling as he let out peals of delighted laughter. Ull tickled his tummy with a soft daffodil from the garden, babbling incoherently at his cherubic face as the little one's brilliant blue eyes lit up in the exact same way his father's did. I watched the vision both from inside and out, my heart swelling with love and pride far beyond its physical capacity. I pulled myself back to the present moment, and looked at my husband with awe. The expression in his eyes made me smile. He had more insight than I gave him credit for.

"Ull?"

"I have been focusing when I see you slip into your visions, and they are still hazy but I am starting to be able to see them with you. I think that was part of the Norn's plan—for me to see what you see, so I can watch out for you. But this is more than I ever let myself hope for." Ull's eyes shone with unshed tears. "You are going to have my baby ..."

"This certainly complicates things, doesn't it?" I murmured, not bothered for some reason by the discovery that my visions were now marital property.

"How will I surprise you with the big news?"

"I missed the timeframe," Ull offered. "How long do we get to practice?"

"Not long." I beamed. "The daffodils were blooming. He'll be a spring baby." I was overwhelmed with happiness.

"Well then, Mrs. Myhr. We had better get started." Ull placed our glasses on the grass and swept the remnants of our picnic to the side. Then he leaned toward me. It took every bit of willpower I had to resist.

"Your parents are waiting for us."

"Kristia, my parents have been waiting for me since I first bought Ýdalir. It has been decades since I have spent any goodly amount of time here. Another hour will not kill them."

"But it's my first time in their home, and I want to be a good guest." I raised my chin.

"All right, sweetheart, but only because this is your first visit to Asgard. On our next trip, you are *all* mine." He looked at me, a lock of that adorably disheveled hair flopping over one eye. I brushed it aside, and the touch of his skin beneath my fingers nearly changed my mind.

"*Jeg elsker deg*," I whispered softly.

"I love you, too, darling." He kissed me gently. We sat beneath the perfect sky, content to be exactly where we were.

All too soon we returned to the Great Hall, now transformed for the celebratory banquet. Polished columns rose from the floor. Long tables filled the room and white banners hung from the high ceilings. There was no excessive décor, no grandiose art or carvings like I would have imagined for a hall of the gods. It was simply a gathering spot for old friends. What made it so remarkable was the feeling within— everyone chatted happily, embracing one another and passing food with hearty laughter. For all its many members, I could see that Asgard was a family home. Ull and I stood at the entrance, hands tightly clasped, and I realized that I was a part of this family, too.

When we walked in, hands clapped our backs and arms stretched out with welcoming hugs. Elsker waved at me from a table filled with equally tiny, white-haired ladies. Though it was my first time at such a banquet, I felt like I'd been here my whole life. Ull kissed my cheek and I gazed up at him adoringly. I was so grateful to him for so many reasons. He had given me family, love, security, and the promise of a lifetime of happiness by his side. I was finally right where I belonged.

❄ ❄ ❄ ❄

After the feast, we approached Odin with our decision to stay on earth. When he offered us residence in Asgard, Ull declined so politely his grandfather took no offense.

"We look forward to visiting often. But to be honest, we have a good thing going where we are. And so long as we are able to keep up with our duties, we would prefer to stay in Midgard," came Ull's gentle rebuff.

Odin took it in stride, and we were granted

indefinite leave to perform our duties as telecommuters.

"Will there be anything else?" Odin looked at me like he knew the answer.

"Actually, sir. There is one thing." I leaned in to whisper my plan.

When I finished, Odin chuckled. "I had a feeling."

"Gunnar agreed to let us try it out, but I haven't talked to Jens yet. I know he worries about Inga being a warrior or a Valkyrie, but this isn't exactly the same thing. And besides, Inga and I are together all the time anyway. So if I ever were attacked, she'd be in the middle of it. You know she wouldn't turn down a good fight." I pleaded my case.

"That is true. I see no reason we cannot at least let Inga be your guard on a trial basis. If we find it is not working, we can reevaluate."

"Oh, thank you!" It took everything I had not to throw my arms around him.

"Just give me a moment."

"Of course." I tugged at Ull's hand and led him a few feet away. He wrapped his arms around my waist from behind and rested his chin on my head.

"I still say it is a long shot," he murmured.

"You also said you'd never bet against Inga," I reminded him.

"True."

"Inga," Odin called. She turned away from her conversation and glided across the room.

"Jens." Odin motioned to his advisor. Jens hurried to his side.

Odin dropped his voice to a murmur, so we were left to guess at the conversation. Jens' mouth drooped in a frown and he shook his head. But after Inga treated him to her puppy-dog look, he nodded. She jumped up and down and hugged her father, and then bounced on her toes as she scanned the room. When her eyes found me she gave me two thumbs up. I returned the gesture with a grin.

Go, I mouthed, waving her toward Gunnar. She turned and ran across the room, nearly tackling him as she jumped into his arms.

"Somebody is happy," Ull whispered in my ear.

"That makes two of us." If I had to have a bodyguard, I was glad it would be one of my best friends.

"So, we are going back to Bibury," Ull confirmed.

"Yep." I leaned back into him as he wrapped his arms tighter around me.

"You do not mind, do you Olaug?" Ull spotted her at a table nearby, chatting with Elsker, Sif and Thor. He pulled me over to her.

"Mind what, my boy?"

"Going back to Midgard?"

"I never mind going there." Her eyes crinkled. "Has Odin approved?"

"Yes." I grinned. "And Inga's going to be my bodyguard."

"Oh, how wonderful for you both." There was genuine pleasure in Olaug's eyes. She knew how long Inga had wanted a position like this.

"What about you, Elsker? Where will you settle

now?" I turned to the tiny woman.

"Why, Bibury, of course. I'll want to spend lots of time with the baby." She winked at me.

"Baby!" Sif squealed from her seat.

"Baby? What baby? Kristia, are you pregnant?" Olaug jumped up.

"Not yet," I hissed. "Elsker, you can't go around doing that!"

"I am a Norn." She waved her hand, unconcerned. "These visions just come to me."

"Well, you don't have to blurt them out." Honestly, nothing was private around here.

"There's going to be a baby!" Olaug was off in another world. She practically skipped toward the Bifrost, babbling giddily about pudgy baby legs and toes.

"I guess we had better follow her." Ull shrugged. "Mother, Father, Please visit often."

"We will, Son." Sif hugged him tightly. "Oh, a baby!"

"Sif," I moaned. Not her too.

"It's just so exciting! Take care of each other." She kissed me on both cheeks.

"Of course. See you soon." I shook Thor's hand.

"Absolutely."

"Gunnar! Inga!" Ull called across the room. "Are you ready?"

They sauntered over to us, hand in hand. Inga's eyes were bright. "Let's go."

"Elsker." Ull leaned toward the Norn as an afterthought. "Do you have any insights about the baby?"

"Hmm." Elsker narrowed her eyes. She stood and put both hands on my stomach. "Ahh. I see."

"What? What do you see?"

"Asgard's little prince will make his appearance before next summer. And he has a very special gift for our realm." Elsker stepped back, her face glowing with happiness.

"Before summer, *ja*?" Ull looked at me.

Oh, great Odin, his parents were *right there*.

"Come, darling. I need to get you home. Now." He placed his hands on my hips and ushered me toward the Bifrost. I heard the laughter behind us but I was too mortified to look.

"Heimdall, Bibury, please." Ull instructed the gatekeeper as we caught up to Olaug. Inga and Gunnar piled in with us, and once again I had the uncomfortable sensation of traveling through the realms. I was more than a little relieved when my feet touched the grassy meadow behind Ýdalir.

"We've got some house hunting to do. Olaug, you're coming with us. The lovebirds need some privacy." Inga dragged Gunnar and Olaug off in the direction of town. The one realtor in our village wouldn't know what had hit her.

"It would seem we have Ýdalir to ourselves, Mrs. Myhr." Ull grabbed my waist and pulled me close, leaving no room for questions. I breathed in his heady scent, intoxicated by his nearness. I stroked one substantial bicep, looking up, up, up until my eyes finally reached his. His mouth was pulled into that adorable half-smile and I reached up to brush the stray lock of hair from his eyes. My insides turned soft. He grabbed my wrist and pulled it to his chest. Then he kissed me. Hard.

I pulled away, breathless. "What did you have in mind?"

The smolder in his eyes grew and he swept me off my feet, running past the startled sheep grazing in the meadow. The movement was surprisingly smooth, but despite his graceful sprint the butterflies in my belly took flight, as if someone had jabbed them with a branding iron. In an instant my hands were in Ull's hair, pulling his face to mine. My lips peppered hot kisses along his jawline, the coarse fibers of his perma-stubble scraping my sensitive skin. I didn't care. I wasn't acting on any logical level anymore. My entire being was consumed with the overwhelming need to be Ull's, in every conceivable way. And if my lips endured a few abrasions in the meantime, it would be more than worth it.

Besides, that stubble was sexy as all Helheim.

Ull bolted through the back gate as my teeth grazed his earlobe. He let out a shudder, the tremble rocking through his body and resonating where his arms wrapped around the backs of my legs. He set his jaw and ran faster, not bothering to close the French doors after he ripped them open. I shifted in his arms, pulling myself higher so I could trace the top of his ear with my tongue. The butterflies flapped harder as Ull put one hand on my hip. He swung my legs free and I wrapped them around his waist. Now I clung to him, legs cinched tightly around him like a belt, and arms twined around his neck. He moved one hand to the small of my back, fisting my hair with the other. As he neared our bedroom, he turned so he ran in reverse. He slammed his back against the door, sending wood chips flying.

"Ull!" I giggled. "You broke it!"

"Not exactly my concern right now, sweetheart." Ull dove for the bed, cradling me in his arms to cushion the fall. He landed with a soft thud, then rolled onto his back.

I pushed myself up on my elbows and gazed adoringly at my real-life Norse god. My fingers traced the outline of his mouth and he parted his lips, sucking lightly on the pad of my thumb. His tongue was hot, and it sent a surge through my body, making me flush in a way that wasn't remotely unpleasant. As I stared at the pale pink skin of his lips, he turned his head, teeth raking my skin.

"Breathe," he reminded me. I sucked in air like I was drowning. In a way, I was. There was a very real possibility I could stay lost in this moment forever.

"Kiss me," I demanded. Ull's eyes shifted to my favorite shade as he threw his arm across my back. Before I could take a second breath, he was on top of me, the full weight of his massive frame pressing me into the soft down of the mattress. An involuntary sigh escaped me as Ull covered my mouth with a commanding kiss. His tongue pushed at my lips, exploring every surface with a frenzied need. I felt like I was about to burst out of my own skin. My nails scraped against the muscles of his back as I tugged his sweater over his head, throwing it somewhere on the floor. Or maybe it was on the nightstand. I didn't care. I wanted—no, I needed to be as close to Ull as possible. Now.

He raised himself on one elbow and pulled his T-shirt off. The movement made him press against me in a way that sent my head spinning. My torso tensed as I willed him to hurry up. The twinkle in his inky blue eyes made it clear my message came through.

"Once a mortal." He chuckled. "Still impatient?"

I was too distracted to respond. Ull was right there, in all his shirtless glory. The muscles of his shoulders jutted out, and his biceps bulged as he shifted his weight again. It was more than any girl could handle. I turned my head to kiss the hard surface of his tricep, then slowly made my way up his arm. Ull groaned when I moved to his neck. He put his hand under my head and tugged at my hair. I reluctantly pulled away, my eyes wide.

"Before we do this." Ull paused. He sat back on his knees, and stared down at me. His hands moved slowly across my stomach, his fingers drawing a light pattern along my ribs. A searing heat that ran all the way to the tips of my toes immediately replaced the shiver that wracked my torso. *Gods, he needs to hurry this up.* I was about ten seconds away from spontaneous deific combustion.

"Before we do this," Ull repeated. He reached the bottom of my sweater and slid his fingers under the fabric. Searing heat became an unbearable inferno. I squirmed, but Ull continued at his own languid pace.

He moved his fingers up my burning abdomen, and finally lifted the sweater over the top of my head. My head fell back on the pillow as my breath came in ragged gasps.

"Oh my God, before we do this, *what*? What? You know you're *killing* me right now." My voice came out as a whimper.

"You are immortal." Ull winked. I whipped my head to the side and buried my face in the pillow so I couldn't yell at him. No matter what I was, if he didn't finish this *right now* I was going to explode.

"Before we do this," Ull said for the third agonizing time, "I was thinking. For our son's name, how do you feel about . . ." He leaned down and brushed his lips against my ear, whispering something so sweet that I smiled in spite of my frustration.

"I love it." I turned to stare into Ull's eyes. They were endless, deep, twinkling orbs that only skimmed the surface of his beautiful soul and stretched into the depths of forever.

Just like our future.

But it wasn't the time to focus on our tomorrows. My very own Norse god commanded my full attention. As he would, thanks to the interference of a well-intentioned Norn, for the rest of our existence.

CHAPTER SEVENTEEN

"DO NOT LIFT THAT!" Ull jumped in front of me and picked up the box. "You have to take care of yourself. This is too heavy for you."

A month had passed, and I was absolutely thrilled that Elsker and I had been right—I was carrying Ull's baby! Inga and Gunnar had bought the cottage next door, and Bibury's resident domestic goddess was helping me prepare a care package to mail to Ardis. She'd fallen in love with all things British on her European vacation, and was going through major McVitie's withdrawals now that she was back in New York. I placed a strip of tape along the edge of the packing box. It was filled with Caramel Digestives, Hobnobs, and an array of English teas. The entire thing weighed five, maybe six pounds, tops. It was totally manageable for a human to handle, and even easier for a goddess.

However, my overprotective husband thought I had the constitution of an orchid.

"Ull," I protested. "I may be pregnant but I can lift five pounds. Honest."

"This is more like ten." Ull easily raised the package with two fingers. "I know you think I am being overbearing, but I do not want you hurting yourself. Or our precious cargo." He set the box on the counter and cradled my belly with both hands. "*Hei hei*, little one." He kneeled so his face was level with my stomach. "Daddy loves you so very much. Yes he does. We are going to have so much fun together; do you know that? When you come out I will teach you to play football and rugby and wield a sword, and handle a mace, and—"

"Um, do you know any activities that *won't* require a helmet?" Our son wasn't even born yet and Ull was plotting to rough him up.

"Of course." Ull gave me a dazzling smile and returned to my belly. "We can read stories and sing songs. I cannot wait to kiss your little toes, and your tiny little fingers, my darling baby boy." He kissed my stomach and looked up at me tenderly. "Thank you for giving me a son."

I tousled his hair. "Thank you for making me your wife. I'm glad we're growing."

"Me, too. You two are my world."

"I know. But I promise I won't hurt either of us if I carry some cookies in a basket."

Ull frowned as he stood. "Nonetheless. Inga," he gestured, "you will carry this for her."

"Aye aye, Captain." She saluted with a giggle. "Can we go now?"

"Are you sure you do not want me to come with you? It is a long way to the post office."

"It is one-point-four miles. I'll be fine. The scariest thing I could encounter in Bibury is an errant cow."

"An errant cow can be plenty dangerous," Ull muttered darkly. "If one had not fed Ymir, we would not have jotuns, or fire giants, or . . . forget it. I am coming with you."

"No, Ull. It's fine. You're working. And I'll have Inga with me. She's the most formidable woman I know, Sif excluded."

"All right," Ull acquiesced. "But take your mobile. If you feel at all uncomfortable, ring me and I will be right there."

"I know." I stood on tiptoe to kiss him. "I love you, my sweet, overbearing husband."

"And I you, my beguiling, stubborn wife."

We kissed as Inga picked up the cookies that had caused so much contention. "Now may we leave, or do you want to put a GPS tracker on her?"

"Inga," I chided, before adding sheepishly, "You know, there's one on my phone." *Stupid fancy new phone.* My flip phone mysteriously 'disappeared' the day Ull found out I was pregnant.

"Sorry. Ull, I promise to take care of your wife and baby if you grant me leave from your castle." She gave her sweetest expression.

"Get out of here, Inga." Ull cuffed her shoulder as he headed back to his library.

"Ull?" I called after him.

He turned.

"Let me know if there's any news on Loki, okay?" The monster's trial had been a short one, and Odin was expected to deliver his verdict that afternoon. If Loki got anything less than a life imprisonment, Ull and I would need to leave immediately to search for the cure for Olaug. Neither of us wanted to undertake our search for the lost artifact while I was pregnant. Not to mention that we didn't want to worry about Loki ever getting near our child. A lifetime sentence would kill two birds with one stone.

The outcome I was rooting for wasn't exactly charitable.

Ull nodded. "You know I will. But do not worry about Loki. It is not good for the baby."

"Thank you, Dr. Myhr," I teased.

"Any time. Be safe, my love."

I blew him a kiss and turned to leave. Inga shook her head as we closed the front door behind us. "Boy, never thought I'd see the day Asgard's fiercest assassin talked to a tummy."

"Tell me about it. You know he sings to the baby at night," I confided.

"No!" Inga's eyes popped.

"It's really cute. Little lullabies in Norwegian. He rubs my belly and sings for a good half hour." Of course, I had pretty much no idea what he was singing. I quickly added *learn better Norwegian* to my list of nesting activities.

We walked down the drive of Ýdalir. We traveled

223

a half-mile down the road, stopping to watch the sheep cross and waving at the farmer who kept them on their path.

"Are you having a nice afternoon, Mrs. Russotti?" I asked. Antonia Russotti was a charming woman in her early eighties, with perfectly coiffed white hair and laugh lines around her eyes. My grandmother would have loved her—even in slacks and muddy wellies, Mrs. Russotti always wore her pearls.

"I am. How are you ladies today?"

"We're well. We're posting a care package to a friend in the States. Do you need anything from the post office?"

"Actually, I could use a book of stamps."

"We can get them for you," I offered.

"That would be wonderful. Thank you, girls. How about you bring them by tomorrow and I'll have a fresh batch of cannoli for the both of you? Bring Olaug, too. I haven't seen her in weeks. What has she been up to?" Mrs. Russotti tilted her head.

"Oh, a little of this, a little of that." I waved my hand. "You know Olaug, she's not so great with idle time. Always a busy bee."

Beside me, Inga let out a delicate snort.

"Do bring her. I've missed her stories. And we can show our new neighbor here the birds." Mrs. Russotti smiled at Inga.

"They're really neat," I agreed. "Mrs. Russotti has a lovely aviary filled with yellow canaries."

"Ooh." Inga grinned. "I can't wait."

"See you around three, then?"

I nodded. "Yes ma'am. Um, Mrs. Russotti." I glanced down the lane where one of her flock had taken a wrong turn. "You've got a runner."

"Oops. See you tomorrow, girls." Mrs. Russotti took off after the errant sheep, and Inga and I continued on our walk.

"Are you excited about redoing the London house?" Inga asked.

"I really am. It will be fun to live there for a while. And I can't wait to see Emma and Victoria again. They're both working in the city this summer—Emma's at an economics consulting firm, and Victoria's over at Alexander McQueen." I smiled.

Ull and I had talked it over, and I'd decided to take a leave of absence from school. Becoming immortal, learning to control the elements, carrying Ull's baby, *and* taking a full course-load was as more than I felt I could comfortably handle—even as a goddess. Instead, Ull and I were going to spend the next few months turning our Kensington row house into a family home. We planned to add a nursery to the top story, and convert part of the second floor into a playroom. Spending time with my girlfriends would make the summer just that much more perfect.

"And Ull is going to let us traipse off to London to oversee these renovations? You *are* bringing your bodyguard with you, *ja*?"

I laughed. "You can stay in Bibury and enjoy what's left of your summer with Gunnar. Ull's coming with me—I guess he had Olaug network the London house so he can work remotely."

"Figures," Inga muttered. "You know he's making me redundant."

"I'm sorry." I patted her arm. "But you can always come visit! Think of the shopping you could do in London."

"Hmm." Inga's eyes sparkled. "Think of the things we could buy for the baby. We need a crib, and a pram, and a rocking horse . . ."

My mind spiraled into baby-brain mode, imagining tiny little booties and hats. And before I knew it we were at the post office.

"Good morning, Inga. Hi Kristia." The woman behind the counter tossed her wavy, brown hair over her shoulder as she greeted me with a fond smile. "I was just about to ring you—something came for you this morning."

"Really? How funny. I just came in to mail this, and buy a book of stamps." I smiled at Mrs. Dillin as Inga placed Ardis's package on the counter. The woman weighed it, and I paid for the postage. Ardis would be one happy girl, in seven to ten days' time.

"I'll just be two shakes." Mrs. Dillin ducked out and returned with a small parcel. "Here you are."

"Thank you, ma'am." My hands closed around the package.

"Don't forget your stamps." Mrs. Dillin picked up a small booklet and handed it to Inga. She slid it into her back pocket.

"Thank you so much. Have a good day, Mrs. Dillin!" Inga waved over her shoulder. She turned to me as we closed the door behind us. "What'd you get?"

"I don't know." I turned the parcel over. My lips drew up as I recognized the return address. "Ardis."

Inga peered over my shoulder. "But that says it came from Nehalem. She's back in New York."

"I know. Must be from her parents." With a tear, I opened the padded envelope. My fingers felt inside until I pulled out a piece of paper. My pace slowed as I took in Ardis's mom's loopy scrawl. The writing took me back to afternoons in the Behrman kitchen, where plates of cookies flanked by handwritten notes informed us that Mrs. Behrman had run to the market, and would be back soon.

I skidded to a stop and Inga followed suit. "What's it say?"

"It says . . . um . . ." My eyes read through the page. "Huh."

"What?"

"Ardis's dad was my grandmother's attorney. He found something of Mormor's in his safety deposit box—I guess she gave it to him for safekeeping, and he didn't find it until a few weeks ago." I turned the envelope over and shook out its contents. A small silver ring slid out. It was plain, with a delicate blue stone in the center. "That's pretty. The note says it was an heirloom. Wonder where it's from."

I turned the band over in my fingers and it emitted a long flash. Then it freed itself from my grasp, and hovered an inch above my still-pinched-together fingers.

Well, it wasn't the strangest thing I'd seen that summer.

Inga grabbed my arm. "Do you know what that is?" she hissed.

"I'm guessing it's not the heirloom Mormor told Mr. Behrman it was?" I hissed back.

Inga grabbed the ring out of the air and hustled me down the road. "Get that thing out of sight or all Helheim will break loose."

"Okay." I shook my arm free as she steered me back to Ýdalir. "I can walk on my own!"

"Hurry." Inga marched at a clipped pace.

My steps matched hers as we sped back to Ýdalir. We crossed beneath the arch of trees and walked past the fountain without so much as a glance at the splashing fish. When we reached the steps, Inga all but shoved me inside and closed the blue door behind her.

CHAPTER EIGHTEEN

"HEI HEI **DARLING. LITTLE** one. Inga." Ull came out of the library, running a hand through his hair. He crossed the living area and swept me up in his arms. "I missed you so much." He gingerly ran a hand over my belly before kissing me with a force I wasn't expecting. I wrapped my arms around his neck and kissed back, giving in to the hormones surging through my body.

Ull chuckled. "I like you pregnant."

"Me too. Why'd you stop?"

"Because I am wondering what is wrong with Inga."

Our friend paced the entryway like a caged chipmunk.

"I have no idea." I shrugged. "But it has something to do with my new ring. Old ring. The ring."

"Who gave you a ring?" Ull squinted.

"My grandmother? I think."

"Your grandmother passed away." Ull stared at

Inga. "What is going on?"

"This." Inga stopped pacing long enough to point the ring at Ull. "Kristia got this in the mail."

Ull sucked in a sharp breath. "Where did it come from?"

"Here." I offered the envelope and the note. Ull read it quickly.

"Ardis's parents sent this to you?"

"Yes." I took back the note. "Mr. Behrman was Mormor's attorney, and it sounds like she asked him to hold this for me."

"Why is he only sending it to you now? Your grandmother died two years ago." Ull raised an eyebrow.

"I don't know. The note says he just found it. Though how it could have disappeared from a safety deposit box is beyond me." Even in Nehalem, those things were locked up tighter than a clam with lockjaw.

"May I see it?" Ull held out his hand and Inga dropped the ring into it. The silver band rested calmly in his palm. "It is not working."

"Of course it's not." Inga rolled her eyes. "Have Kristia hold it."

Ull nodded and I took the ring between my pointer and index fingers. As I did, it emitted a sharp beam of light. I loosened my grip and the ring floated on its own. My gaze darted between Inga and Ull. They were both staring at the floating object as if they'd seen a ghost.

"No," Ull whispered. "It has been missing for

decades."

"It's been missing since Kjell defected." Inga gave Ull a pointed look. "You know what this means."

My hand shot into the air. "I don't know what this means."

Ull plucked the ring out of the air. With a gentle touch to the small of my back, he guided me to the couch. "Inga, would you get her some water?"

Inga nodded, and flew into the kitchen. She came back seconds later, with three glasses and a plate of scones.

"How'd you know I was hungry?" I took a pastry.

"You're pregnant." Inga shrugged.

Ull rubbed my leg softly as I bit into the scone. While I chewed, he took the note out of my hand. "Hmm. I did not see that coming."

"Me neither. But we should have known the Three Sisters wouldn't have cast the Seer from a pure mortal. No offense." Inga shot me a look.

"What is going on?" I was trying to be patient, but this was getting weird. And in this crowd, that said a lot.

"Kristia." Ull set the note down and turned his attention to me. He held both of my hands in his. "That letter says the ring is a family heirloom. That it was a gift to your maternal ancestor from her husband, Kjell."

"So why is my family heirloom floating? And why is Inga acting so weird?"

"Because it is not a family heirloom from your mortal side. It is an heirloom from your Asgardian

231

side." Ull didn't break eye contact.

"I don't have an Asgardian side. I mean, I do now, obviously. But I didn't six months ago. And I didn't two years ago, or whenever Mormor left this ring with Mr. Behrman."

"Yes you did." Ull gently rubbed the tops of my hands with his thumbs. "When we were dating and I wanted to become a human so we could be together, I told you about a god who had left Asgard to marry a mortal. Do you remember?"

"Vaguely." Ull's threat to give up his immortality was something I tried not to think about anymore.

"His name was Kjell. He was a warrior, and he fell in love with a mortal on a routine peacekeeping mission to Midgard. He approached Odin and asked that she be granted admission to Asgard, but Odin refused to create an immoral. He said it went against the laws of the realms.

"Kjell left Asgard, and never returned. He relinquished his immortality, married the mortal, and eventually died a Midgardian. He got to spend his life with the woman he loved, and by all accounts he got the life he wanted. But Odin was furious. He never believed Kjell would really leave. He was one of Odin's finest warriors—captained the Elite Team for twenty cycles, and held a kill record that was only recently topped. Losing him was the impetus Odin needed to create the test that allowed you to join our family."

"So Kjell moved to Earth and married the mortal? What happened to them?" I asked.

Ull's eyes twinkled. "Jens watched them for a few

years. Kjell found work as a fisherman, and set up a home with his bride not far from where you used to live, in Oregon. After a few years, he and the mortal had a baby. Jens watched for a bit more, to see if the baby displayed any supernatural gifts. It appeared she was as human as her mother, and so it was decided the happy family could live out their days without Asgardian supervision."

"So you don't know what happened to Kjell's family after that?"

"We did not. Until now." Ull tapped the note. "Your grandmother was in possession of a ring that belonged to Kjell. The note said it was a family heirloom, a gift from your great-great-great-great-great grandfather to his bride."

"Which means . . ." My stomach fluttered.

Ull held my gaze. "It means you were never fully human. The Asgardian genes were depleted by a few generations of mortal pairings, not to mention Kjell's relinquishment of his immortality, but the reason you had visions all your life; the reason you felt so drawn to our world; the reason Elsker chose you for me . . . it is because you are Kjell's descendant."

It was a full minute before I was able to blink.

"I was never fully human."

"No."

"And this ring . . ."

"It's the Healing Stone," Inga offered helpfully. "Kjell won it from a fire giant in battle, and he took it with him when he left Asgard."

"The Healing Stone. It's the lost artifact that can

233

help Olaug." My voice broke.

"It can. But it can only be activated by its rightful owner." Ull squeezed my hands.

"But I'm not its owner: Kjell is. Was. Whatever. Why does it float for me and not for you guys? You're more Asgardian than I am. Was. Arugh." I shook my head.

"Because the ring does not belong to us. Magic dictates that an object is loyal to whomever creates or captures it, so long as the transfer is final. Kjell won the stone from the giant, thereby winning its fealty. And he put that fealty to good use. Your great-great-great grandfather knew that once he relinquished his immortality, he would be vulnerable to all sorts of attacks. Asgard's enemies would track him down and kill both him and his bride on sight. Taking down a god, even a retired one, would be a great prize. And while he was not concerned for his own fate, he wanted to protect the woman he loved. So Kjell asked the light elves to make the stone into a ring for his bride. It would not be able to stave off death by natural causes, but it would protect against supernatural elements—enchanted weapons, curses, crushing spells." Ull raised an eyebrow. "When Kjell reached Midgard, he gifted the ring to his wife and its fealty transferred to her. She must have passed it to her child in her will. And she to hers. And so on. Until it became your grandmother's. And now, yours."

I stared at the ring as it lay on the coffee table. It twinkled at me.

"So, not only am I the Seer, but I have a magic

healing ring, too?"

"Yes." Inga clapped her hands. "You know what this means?"

I let out a breath. "Olaug's going to be okay."

"Exactly." Ull nodded. "When you put on the ring, you will be able to imbue anything you touch with therapeutic properties."

"So our baby . . ." I rubbed my stomach.

"Will be healthy as a Pegasus." Ull kissed the top of my head.

"A doctor for a father and a healer for a mother. Plus you can see what he's going to do before he does it? Poor kid's going to have *no* fun in high school." Inga giggled.

"Sweetheart, are you all right? Your forehead feels warm." Ull held the back of his hand to my face.

"It's never ending, is it? Just when I think I have a grip on this life, there's a whole new twist. It's kind of crazy."

"There is definitely something new every day," Ull agreed.

"So I'll be able to protect our baby from Loki, and dark elves, and jotuns, and . . . well, all the things," I mused. "And I'll be able to protect you guys if, Odin forbid, we're ever cursed. But first we need to take care of Olaug."

"Already on it." Inga typed into phone. When it beeped, she nodded. "She's on her way upstairs."

My stomach churned. "How do I know what to do? This ring didn't exactly arrive with a manual."

"It will just come to you," Olaug's voice came from

the doorway. She tottered into the living area and sat beside me on the couch. "Put the ring on."

The ring rose from the table and floated to my right hand. It hovered, waiting for me to unclench my fist. I gulped. "Okay."

The minute the ring was on, I felt a surge of energy. It pulsed from my hand to my heart, and back again. Cool air hit the whites of my eyes as my brows shot up. "It feels . . . weird," I whispered.

"Bet you've felt weirder," Inga pointed out.

I shuddered. There was no need to revisit Idunn's little procedure.

"Now place your hand over my heart," Olaug instructed.

My fingers shook as I rested my palm against Olaug's heart. The energy pushed away from me now, from my heart, down my arm, and out through the ring. The blue stone glowed, and nine beams emitted from its center. I jumped at the ring's sudden outburst. It was brighter than the midday sun on Asgard Cay, and the way it moved energy through my body left me feeling like I'd just downed an entire case of energy drinks. I took a deep breath and kept my hand against Olaug's chest. My palm vibrated against Olaug's ribcage, filling her body with light. When the light dimmed, I pulled my hand back.

Holy mother of pearl. This life was crazy.

"Did it work? How do you feel?" I held my breath.

Olaug flexed her hands experimentally. Then she stood, and turned in a slow circle. "I feel . . . wonderful. The pain is gone."

"Are you certain?" Ull stared at Olaug.

"I am certain." She nodded. "Well done, Kristia."

My voice shook. "I'm not entirely sure what I did, but I'm glad it worked."

Ull turned to me. He rested his large hand on my belly. "How are the two of you?"

"We're fine." I stroked his jaw. "And thanks to Kjell's ring, it looks like we're going to be fine for a long time."

Ull drew me to him, wrapping strong arms around my shoulders. "If any of this is too much for you, just say the word and I will take you and the baby away. It is wonderful that you have this gift, but if it interferes with you or our child's happiness, I will make all of this disappear."

"I can handle it." I lay my cheek against Ull's chest. "Do you honestly think I'd back away from something like this?"

"I wish I could say yes." Ull shook his head. "But if there is one thing I know about you, it is that you love a challenge."

"Not half as much as I love you."

"I can see we're not needed here any more. Olaug? Walk me home?" I heard Inga and Olaug's laughter as they closed the door behind them, but I didn't see them leave. My eyes were locked on Ull's perfect face: the strong line of his jaw, the sparkling orbs of his eyes, and the pale pink lips that lowered themselves onto mine. Ull kissed a trail from my mouth down the side of my neck and I melted.

"It seems we have an evening of celebrating ahead

of us."

"Mmm. What did you have in mind?"

"How about dinner in the garden? Grilled steaks, twice-baked potatoes, and fresh green beans, courtesy of your doting husband." He nibbled his way up to my chin.

"I like the sound of that."

"And for dessert, fresh apple cobbler. You will need your strength for phase two of our celebration." He breathed on my ear and I shivered.

"I can't wait," I whispered. I brushed my lips against Ull's, kissing him soundly. He was only too happy to give in as he picked me up, and started running. I couldn't help but laugh as he raced down the hallway. And once again I marveled at the amazing turns my life had taken since Ull Myhr dropped into it.

"You know something?" I gazed up at him and twirled a lock of his hair around one finger. "*Jeg elsker deg*."

"I love you too, darling." Ull beamed down at me, and closed the bedroom door behind us.

I let out a soft sigh and traced the line of his jaw with one finger. This god, this life: it was everything I had ever wanted. I was absolutely overwhelmed with gratitude.

"*Jeg elsker deg*," I whispered again. "Forever."

He winked, then kissed me softly. "Forever."

ACKNOWLEDGMENTS

To the cutie-pie who gives me the world every single day. *Jeg elsker deg*. Forever. To our little gentlemen—for teaching me to live fully within each moment and for filling my heart with more love than I ever thought possible. You are the pinnacle of *tro*. I'm so grateful God gave me you.

To Lauren McKellar and Eden Plantz, two of the finest editors in all the realms; and to Stacey Nash, the voice of reason and happiness. Thank you for making these little journal stories shine.

To the RagnaRockstars, to my writer friends, and to everyone who gave the thousand-and-one pep talks. *Tusen takk*. For all the things.

To the readers who embrace these re-imagined myths—I'm humbled and thankful that you choose to take these crazy journeys with me. None of this could happen without you, and I am so very grateful.

To Imagine Dragons, Peet's Coffee, Alexander Skarsgård, the makers of McVitie's Caramel Digestives, and Gunnar's mom. Because, reasons. And to MorMorMa. Always.

ABOUT THE AUTHOR

Before finding domestic bliss in suburbia, S.T. Bende lived in Manhattan Beach (became overly fond of Peet's Coffee) and Europe...where she became overly fond of McVitie's cookies. Her love of Scandinavian culture and a very patient Norwegian teacher inspired her YA Fantasy series. She hopes her characters make you smile, and she dreams of skiing on Jotunheim and Hoth.

Find S.T. on her website at www.stbende.com, or subscribe to her newsletter at http://smarturl.it/BendeNewsletter.

WANT MORE OF THE NORSE CREWS?

Meet the God of Winter and his Norse crew in
THE ELSKER SAGA.
THE ELSKER SAGA: TUR (a novella)
THE ELSKER SAGA: ELSKER
THE ELSKER SAGA: ENDRE
THE ELSKER SAGA: TRO
THE ELSKER SAGA: COMPLETE BOXED SET

Meet the God of War and his Norse crew in
THE ÆRE SAGA.
THE ÆRE SAGA: PERFEKT ORDER
THE ÆRE SAGA: PERFEKT CONTROL
THE ÆRE SAGA: PERFEKT BALANCE

See the crews together in the bonus Elsker/Ære
crossover novella . . .
SUPERNATURAL CHRONICLES: THE ASGARDIANS

And meet the demigods in
NIGHT WAR SAGA.
NIGHT WAR SAGA: PROTECTOR
NIGHT WAR SAGA: DEFENDER
NIGHT WAR SAGA: REDEEMER

Want to know more about Gunnar's brother, Henrik, and Asgard's war god, Tyr? Find out what the *other* Norse crew was up to during the Elsker Saga in . . .

THE ÆRE SAGA: PERFEKT ORDER

All's fair when you're in love with War.

For seventeen-year-old Mia Ahlström, a world ruled by order is the only world she allows. A lifetime of chore charts, to-do lists and study schedules have helped earn her a spot at Redwood State University's engineering program. And while her five year plan includes finding her very own happily-evah-aftah, years at an all-girls boarding school left her feeling woefully unprepared for keg parties and co-ed extracurricular activities.

So nothing surprises her more than catching the eye of Tyr Fredriksen at her first college party. The imposing Swede is arrogantly charming, stubbornly overprotective, and runs hot-and-cold in ways that defy reason...until Mia learns that she's fallen for the Norse God of War; an immortal battle deity hiding on Midgard (Earth) to protect a valuable Asgardian treasure from a feral enemy. With a price on his head, Tyr brings more than a little excitement to Mia's rigidly controlled life. Choosing Tyr may be the biggest distraction—or the greatest adventure—she's ever had.

Find out more about PERFEKT ORDER and other books by S.T. Bende at www.stbende.com. Skål!

CPSIA information can be obtained
at www.ICGtesting.com
Printed in the USA
BVHW031934240921
617509BV00011B/55

9 781502 701305